LOVE ON WHEELS

"Would it make you nervous if I watched you and Steve work on your routine tomorrow?" Kyle asked hesitantly.

Holly laughed. "If I haven't gotten used to people watching me skate by now, I'd better give up! When Steve and I are finished practicing, why don't you and I plan to have a lesson of our own?"

"I'd like that," he said, taking her hand. "Thanks for a great time, Holly." To her surprise, Kyle bent down and gave her a tender kiss on the lips before he turned and strode to his car.

Holly stood on the porch, waving as he drove away. Then she touched her mouth. She had been kissed before, but there was something different about this particular kiss. Was it the *way* he had kissed her, or was it Kyle himself that made it so special?

Bantam Sweet Dreams romances
Ask your bookseller for the books you have missed

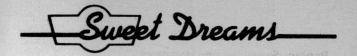

LOVE ON WHEELS

Sandy Jones

BANTAM BOOKS
NEW YORK • TORONTO • LONDON • SYDNEY • AUCKLAND

RL 6, age 11 and up

LOVE ON WHEELS
A Bantam Book / May 1993

*Sweet Dreams and its associated logo are registered
trademarks of Bantam Books, a division of Bantam
Doubleday Dell Publishing Group, Inc. Registered in U.S.
Patent and Trademark Office and elsewhere.*

Cover photo by Pat Hill

ISBN 0-553-29981-6

Published simultaneously in the United States and Canada

*Bantam Books are published by Bantam Books, a division
of Bantam Doubleday Dell Publishing Group, Inc. Its trademark, consisting of the words "Bantam Books" and the por-
trayal of a rooster, is Registered in U.S. Patent and
Trademark Office and in other countries. Marca Registrada.
Bantam Books, 1540 Broadway, New York, New York
10036.*

PRINTED IN THE UNITED STATES OF AMERICA

OPM   0 9 8 7 6 5 4 3 2 1

LOVE
ON WHEELS

Chapter One

The sound of the final bell at the end of the school day caused a flurry of activity in Mrs. Olson's American history class. Textbooks slammed shut and voices rose as the students gathered up their belongings and stampeded for the door.

Holly Benson shoved her class notes between the pages of her history book and joined the kids pouring out of the room. When she finally reached the corridor, it was so crowded that it seemed to take her forever to reach her locker. Holly's best friend, Beth Daniels, was impatiently waiting there.

"What took you so long?" Beth asked, running a hand through the short brown hair that framed her round face. "I'd just about given up on you. What happened? Did Mrs. Olson lock you in the classroom?"

Holly laughed as she opened her locker. "No, but I got caught in a major traffic jam in the hall. We won't be late for practice." Taking out a notebook and her coat, she added, "Mom's driving today since my car's in the shop. She won't leave without us."

When Holly and Beth left the building through the big double doors, they spotted Mrs. Benson's blue sedan in the school parking lot. They hurried down the steps and ran over to the car.

Holly greeted her mother with a big smile. "I hope you haven't been waiting too long," she said as she opened the rear door on the driver's side, letting Beth hop in first.

"No, only about five minutes," Mrs. Benson said.

"That's not true," Holly's seven-year-old brother, Jeffrey, announced from the front seat. "We've been waiting for hours and *hours*." He scrambled up on his knees and turned around, sticking his tongue out at the girls.

"Jeffrey, sit down and put your seat belt back on," his mother said sternly.

Holly reached over the seat and patted Jeffrey's blond head. "Hey, champ. Want to go roller-skating with us?"

"No! I want to play with my friends."

"There will be plenty of time for that after we drop your sister and Beth at the rink," Mrs. Benson said, pulling the car out of the lot and joining the flow of traffic on the street.

Holly and Beth had been best friends ever since third grade when they had both started taking roller-skating lessons. Since then, they had competed in many meets. Sometimes they even competed against each other, but their friendship had never wavered. Holly's mother sewed most of their skating outfits, and Beth's mother trimmed them, making their costumes sparkle when they performed in competition.

While they waited at a stoplight, a faded green car covered with rust drove up beside them. The roar of its engine drowned out all other sounds. The teenage driver, a handsome, dark-haired boy, honked and waved, and Holly smiled and waved back.

The green car pulled away as the light changed, leaving a cloud of black, foul-smelling exhaust in its wake.

"Who was that, dear?" Holly's mother asked as she drove on. "A friend of yours?"

"Kind of. His name's Kyle Evans. He's new

in town, and he has a part-time job at the rink," Holly said.

She had met him the first week of classes after winter break. Kyle had just moved to Linville, and he had asked Holly to help him find his algebra class. They introduced themselves, and from then on whenever they passed each other in the halls, Kyle always made a point of waving and talking to Holly. Her heart beat a little faster when he did, and she had been secretly pleased that Coach Gibson had hired him to work as a general handyman at the rink where she spent so much time.

"But I can't figure Kyle out," Holly murmured.

Beth looked puzzled. "What do you mean?"

"Well, I get the impression that he'd like to take skating lessons, but something's holding him back. I've seen him practicing jumps and spins when he thinks nobody's around, and he's good. With some help from Coach Gibson, I bet he'd be great."

Before Beth could reply, Mrs. Benson stopped the car opposite the entrance to the skating rink. "Well, here we are," she said. "Dad or I will pick you both up about five o'clock."

"We'll be ready. Thanks, Mom," Holly said.

"Yes, thanks," Beth echoed as they stepped out of the car.

They went into the rink, where several skaters were already skimming around the floor.

"I knew we'd be late," Beth said.

"Good afternoon, ladies," a deep, booming voice said. Holly and Beth looked up into the friendly gray eyes of their coach. He glanced at his watch. "A little behind schedule today, I see." Then he smiled. "Have a good practice, girls," he added as he continued down the hallway, whistling to himself.

"Thank goodness we have an understanding coach," Beth said.

The girls headed for the dressing room to change. As they rounded the corner, Holly almost bumped into a tall, attractive skater with long auburn hair and green eyes. "Oops—sorry, Valerie," she said. "Guess I wasn't watching where I was going."

"That's okay," Valerie answered coolly.

"I wish I could skate as well as Valerie does," Holly said with a sigh, wrapping her practice skirt around her waist.

"I admit she's good," Beth agreed. "But you have a much nicer personality."

"Gee, thanks," Holly said wryly. "But a nice personality doesn't win trophies."

"Well, if I remember right, you have a few of those, too," Beth said, lacing up her skates.

"I know. Still, I'd give almost anything if I

could find the right partner and skate free dance like Valerie and Steve do. I've asked Coach Gibson again and again," Holly said. "But he doesn't seem to think that there are any boys in the club who would make a good partner for me."

Beth giggled. "I'd be glad to share Drew— but *only* on the skating floor!"

Holly shook her head. "You two make a terrific team on and off the floor. There's no way we'd share the same magic you two do." She stood up and rolled her skates back and forth, testing the action of the wheels. "Well, I guess we'd better get to work. We're so late already."

As she circled the shiny plastic floor, Holly felt her muscles become pleasantly relaxed. The wheels of her skates rolled smoothly, making little sound.

Holly loved to skate more than anything else. Gliding around the floor gave her a wonderful sensation of freedom. Most of her friends were skaters, too, and Holly was president of the Linville Skating Club, which they all belonged to.

She also enjoyed helping the younger members learn the various movements. Holly could remember how excited she'd been when she perfected her first jump, and when she won her first trophy. She loved seeing the little kids come home from a competition with trophies of their own.

"Let's get a drink before we go on," Beth said when they had finished their warm-ups. "My mouth is so dry."

While they waited their turn behind a long line of other thirsty skaters, a little girl in a bright pink outfit came up and tugged on Holly's skirt. Holly bent down to the little girl's level. "What can I do for you, Sissy?" she asked.

"Can you help me with my two-foot spin?" Her big brown eyes gazed at Holly in eager anticipation.

"Sure," Holly said, smiling. "Just let me get a drink of water. Then we'll go out on the floor and work on it."

"Oh, boy!" Sissy said excitedly. "Thanks, Holly!" She skated over to the railing and waited for Holly to join her.

"You sure are a pushover," Beth said with a grin. "The munchkins think you're the best."

"I enjoy them. Besides, that's the first spin we all learned when we started, remember?"

They both giggled at the memory.

"What's so funny?" they heard someone ask.

Holly and Beth turned around to see a slender, sandy-haired boy smiling at them.

7

"Drew!" Beth said, surprised. "I didn't think you were coming today."

"I wasn't going to, but I finished at the dentist's sooner than expected, so I decided to come on over and get some practice in. I see you're goofing off as usual."

Beth put her hands on her hips. "Drew Williams, how can you say that? You know I practice almost every day."

"Let's say you're *at the rink* almost every day." He took her hand. "Come on—let's work on some dance numbers."

"But my drink of water!" Beth wailed as Drew pulled her toward the floor.

"Later," he said, slipping an arm around her waist.

Holly shook her head, laughing to herself. After she had taken her turn at the fountain, she noticed that Sissy was still standing by the railing. *I almost forgot about her,* Holly thought. She skated over to where Sissy waited. "Ready?" she asked.

Sissy nodded. They rolled out onto the floor together and found a quiet corner near the railing. Holly spent several minutes showing Sissy the correct movements until she felt that the little girl understood how to do the spin.

"You've got the idea. Now all you need to

do is practice what I've shown you over and over," Holly said.

The little girl bobbed her head up and down, making her short blond curls bounce. "Thanks, Holly. I'm going to practice all night!"

Guess I better do some practicing myself, she thought as Sissy skated off across the floor.

Just then Holly felt a gentle hand on her shoulder. She spun around. "Oh, hi, Kyle. Where did you come from? I thought you were cleaning the rink for tonight's session."

"I was done a little early." He brushed his dark brown hair away from his hazel eyes. There was an awkward pause.

Kyle stared at the floor. "I—I was wondering if you could give me some pointers on my jumps and spins. That is, when you've got the time," he mumbled.

Holly's eyes opened wide in astonishment. She took a step back, bumping against the railing and nearly losing her balance. Kyle reached out and grabbed her arm to steady her. His hand felt warm and strong.

"Are you okay?" he asked.

"Yeah, sure," Holly replied. "You just took me by surprise, that's all."

"I'm sorry. I shouldn't have asked you." He

let go of her arm. "I shouldn't have put you on the spot like that, you being the president of the skating club and all."

"What's that got to do with anything?" Holly said quickly. "I'd be glad to help you. I watched you skate once or twice, and I think you're really good."

Kyle's face flushed. "That's real nice of you, but I'm not a competitive skater."

"You could be. Why aren't you?" The words popped out before Holly could stop them. *What a dumb thing to say*, she thought, blushing, too. Aloud, she said, "I guess I shouldn't have said that. It's none of my business. Tell you what—if I have time to-morrow before the club meeting and you're free, we'll work on some techniques together."

A big grin lit up Kyle's handsome face. "Really?"

"Really," Holly said with an answering grin.

"That would be super! See you then."

He skated off across the floor, leaving Holly staring after him. *He sure does have talent*, she thought. *I wonder why he seems so shy about it?*

Chapter Two

At noon the following day, Holly put her books in her locker and headed for the cafeteria. As she entered Beth ran up to her. "Where have you been?" Beth cried. "I've been looking all over the place for you!"

Holly could tell that her friend was excited about something. She picked up a tray, and the girls fell in line behind several other kids. "I was in class where I was supposed to be. Why? What's up?"

"You mean you haven't *heard*?"

"Heard what?" Holly put a plate of spaghetti and a carton of milk on her tray.

"But it's all over school!"

Holly was growing impatient. "*What's* all over school?"

"About Valerie."

They had reached the end of the line, and Holly paid the woman behind the cash register. Then she looked down at Beth's tray. It was empty. Holly giggled. "Are you on a strict diet or something?"

"I can't *believe* I did that." Beth sighed. "Hold on a minute." She ran back down the line and grabbed the first plate of food she saw, then whisked a piece of chocolate pie from the pastry shelf. Hurrying back to the cashier, she tossed two wadded-up bills at her. "Sorry about that," she said with a sheepish grin.

The girls found a table at the far end of the room. "Now what's this about Valerie?" Holly asked as she sat down.

"You really *haven't* heard, have you?" Beth's eyes glowed with excitement.

"I haven't heard anything at all," Holly told her. "Why don't you tell me what this is all about before you burst?"

Beth plopped into her chair and leaned close to Holly, almost sticking her elbow in her mashed potatoes. "Well, we were in gym class playing volleyball, and Valerie was in the front row. Sarah Cummings was playing on the other side and when she served the

12

ball, Valerie jumped up to spike it. *That's* when it happened!"

Holly groaned. "*What* happened?"

"That's when Valerie fell and broke her ankle," Beth announced.

"Are you sure?" Holly asked. "Maybe it's only a sprain."

"No, the school nurse said she was sure it was broken. Valerie's ankle swelled up like a balloon before she could even get her shoe off."

"That's terrible!" Holly said.

"You know what this means, don't you?" Beth leaned even closer. "Valerie won't be able to skate in the upcoming meet. Coach Gibson's going to have a cow."

Holly's eyes widened. "I never thought of that. What a bummer! Valerie's our best skater, too."

The warning bell for the next class rang, and the girls cleared their trays.

"I'll meet you at your locker after school," Beth called as she ran down the hall to her next class.

Holly hurried in the opposite direction. *What a terrible tragedy for Valerie,* she thought as she entered the home economics room. *I wonder if Steve knows about it yet. He'll be a wreck.*

* * *

At the rink later that afternoon, Holly and Beth quickly changed into their practice clothes. The Skating Club meeting was scheduled to start in forty-five minutes, and Holly hoped she'd have enough time to work with Kyle as she had promised.

The girls joined the other skaters on the floor for their warm-up. As they circled the rink, Drew skated over to them.

"I just heard about Valerie," he said. "Bad news."

"I know," Beth said. "Isn't it terrible?"

"Sure is," Drew replied. "I wonder what Steve will do without his partner."

"I've been thinking the same thing," Holly said.

They skated around the rink a couple of times, speculating on what Coach Gibson might do.

"Guess we better get some practice in," Drew said, looking at his watch.

"Right," Beth agreed, taking his hand. "See you in a little while, Holly."

Holly looked around for Kyle. When she spotted him behind the railing, watching the action on the floor, she skated over to him.

"Hi. Want to practice for a while?" she asked, smiling.

"I don't know . . ." Kyle looked down, rolling one skate back and forth. "I hate to take

14

up your time. I know you have a meet coming up soon."

"Don't worry about it. I'll be ready when the time comes."

"Okay—if you're sure." Kyle climbed through the bars of the railing and stood beside her. "Where should we start?"

"Why don't we go around the floor a few times so you can get the feel of your skates?" she suggested. Kyle took her hand, and Holly felt a tingling sensation all the way up her arm.

As they skated around the floor in silence, Holly noticed that his movements were smooth and strong. She wanted to ask him where he'd learned to skate so well, but this time she kept her mouth shut.

After a few minutes they moved to a quiet spot and practiced several different spins. Holly was absolutely sure, after seeing the way Kyle performed, that he'd taken lessons before. No one could be that good without some excellent coaching. So why was he so reluctant to compete?

Forty minutes later, Kyle looked up at the large clock on the wall. "Guess I better get back to work," he said. "And you have your meeting."

"I didn't realize it was that late," Holly said. "How about the same time tomorrow?"

He grinned. "Fine, if you think you can put up with me."

I could put up with you a lot longer than forty minutes, Holly thought as he skated away.

A whistle blew, and Holly and the other skaters looked up to see Coach Gibson standing at the side of the rink. "Time for club," he shouted. "Everybody off the floor!"

The skaters quickly gathered in the snack bar area. Holly, the other officers, and Coach Gibson sat at a table near the front.

Coach Gibson turned to Holly. "Will the president please bring the meeting to order?"

Holly stood up and rapped her knuckles on the plastic tabletop. "The meeting of the Linville Skating Club will now come to order," she said. Everyone became quiet, focusing their attention on her. "Diane will read the minutes of the last meeting."

A tall, lanky girl with short curly hair and pale brown eyes rose and read from a notebook, then sat back down.

Holly turned to Steve, noticing that he looked very glum. "Steve, will you please give the treasurer's report?"

He mumbled a series of figures detailing various expenses the club had incurred. ". . . leaving a balance of seven hundred forty-nine dollars and twelve cents," he finished.

"Thanks," Holly replied. "Now I'm going to turn the meeting over to Coach Gibson, who will tell us all about our next meet."

The coach stood and looked around the room, a solemn expression on his face. "Before I talk about the meet," he began, "I have some bad news. As a lot of you already know, one of our best skaters, Valerie Sutton, broke her ankle in gym class at school today. She won't be skating in this meet." The younger members of the club hadn't heard about Valerie's accident, and all of them were shocked.

For the next half hour while Coach Gibson talked about the meet, Holly kept glancing over at Steve. She felt really sorry for him. Who could ever take Valerie's place?

The coach ended his speech by saying, "Now, I want you all to get out there and practice hard. Even without Valerie, we want to make a good showing."

As all the kids started heading for the floor, Coach Gibson turned to Steve and Holly. "I want to see you two in my office before you go out to practice," he said.

Startled and a little apprehensive, they followed him into his small, cluttered office.

"Have a seat," he said, pointing to two metal folding chairs in front of his desk. When Holly and Steve obediently sat, he

17

leaned forward and rested his folded arms on the desk top. "What I want to talk to you about is the upcoming meet." Coach Gibson looked at Steve. "It's a crying shame that Valerie won't be able to compete. I'm confident you two would have done well in your division—you always do. But I think I may have a solution to the problem." He shifted his attention to Holly. "Holly, I know you've wanted to do free dance for quite some time." He paused. "How would you like to give it a try with Steve for this meet?"

Holly's blue eyes opened wide in amazement, and she tingled all over with excitement. "I'd love to!" she cried, then glanced at Steve. "That is, if it's okay with you."

He shrugged. "Fine by me. You're a pretty good skater. I think we could do real well, but we'll have to practice hard."

Coach Gibson smiled. "I know you two can do it. You're both mature, responsible skaters. But you *do* understand, Holly, it's only temporary. When Valerie's ankle heals, she and Steve will be skating together again."

Holly nodded. "I understand," she replied. "I'm just grateful for this opportunity."

"I'll continue looking for a permanent partner for you," the coach went on, "but right now there just isn't anyone. In the meantime, Steve, show Holly Valerie's part of the

18

routine. Remember, we don't have much time to put the whole thing together."

Steven nodded. "Yes, sir."

Coach Gibson put his hands behind his head and grinned at them. "Well, what are you two doing sitting here? Go on out there and get to work!"

Holly and Steve quickly stood up. As they reached the door, Holly turned back, smiling from ear to ear. "Thanks, Coach," she said happily.

"You've earned it, Holly. I'm counting on you."

Holly was in a daze as she followed Steve onto the floor. She was excited, but she was also nervous. Would she really be able to skate as well as Valerie? Coach Gibson seemed to think she could. He'd said he was counting on her. She only hoped she wouldn't disappoint him—or herself.

Chapter Three

"This is absolutely the greatest! I'm so thrilled for you, Holly! Aren't *you* thrilled?"

Holly sat in the middle of her bed later that afternoon, munching on a handful of potato chips as she listened to Beth on the other end of the phone.

"I guess so," Holly answered.

"This is your big chance!" Beth continued. "You've been wanting to do free dance for ages."

"I know. I guess I'm a little nervous, that's all. Some of the steps Steve showed me today are really hard. I hope I can master them before we have to skate in front of the judges."

"Of course you will. You can do it," Beth replied confidently. "I have complete faith in you."

"Thanks for the pep talk," Holly said. "I'm glad one of us is so optimistic."

"Oh, come on, Holly! You're not getting cold feet, are you?"

"Not exactly. It's just that—well, everything is happening so fast. I keep pinching myself to see if I'm dreaming."

"What did your parents say when you told them?" Beth asked.

"They seemed real happy about it." Holly moved the potato chips out of her way and flopped over onto her stomach. "Mom said she'll even make me a special dress."

"Terrific! What color is it going to be? You'll probably look just like Cinderella going to the ball."

Holly giggled. "In a skating dress? I hardly think so! Maybe I should wear glass skates, too."

"I just can't wait to see what your costume looks like," Beth rattled on. "Four weeks seems like such a long time."

"Not when you're learning a whole new routine. I'd feel better about it if I had four *months* instead."

There was a loud knock on Holly's door. "Hold on, Beth. Come in," she called.

Jeffrey jerked the door open. "Mom said for you to get off the phone and come downstairs for supper."

"Tell her I'll be right there," Holly told her little brother. "Got to eat," she said to Beth. "See you tomorrow."

As she hung up the phone, Holly glanced at the glass-enclosed trophy case in one corner of her room. Her father had made it for her several years ago. Numerous trophies and medals lined the shelves. Did she have the talent to add the most important trophy of her skating career to the display? Holly hoped so. She lifted her chin with a determined sparkle in her blue eyes. "I can do it," she said out loud. "I know I can." With the determination of a soldier going into battle, she strode to the bedroom door, flung it open, and marched down the stairs.

The next day Holly went through the motions of going to class. She tried to concentrate on what her teachers were saying, but time after time she caught herself daydreaming and her mind refused to stop wandering. The prospect of skating free dance with Steve pushed everything else out of her head. One minute she felt nervous and anxious; the next minute she felt thrilled and excited. The mixture of emotions kept her in a tailspin.

As Holly drove to the rink after school, Beth said, "You're awfully quiet. Are you all right? You really haven't been yourself today."

Holly glanced at her friend, then turned her eyes back to the road. "I just thought of something while I was sitting in history class this afternoon," she said. "With all that's happened in the past twenty-four hours, I almost forgot about something that's pretty important."

"What's that?"

"Kyle," Holly said.

"Kyle? What about him?"

Holly sighed. "What am I going to do? I promised to help him with his skating, remember? I can't just tell him to forget it because I'm too busy. I know Coach Gibson and Steve are counting on me, but so is he."

"I see what you mean," Beth said. "But you *are* too busy."

"Maybe, but I don't want to disappoint Kyle. I've got to figure a way to spend some time with him and practice with Steve, too."

"Why can't you just tell Kyle you'll work with him after the meet's over?" Beth suggested.

"I've thought of that," Holly said slowly. "I guess I could, but I'm afraid he'll think it's a cop-out. He doesn't seem to have a whole lot of confidence."

"Maybe you could ask someone else to

help him for a while, at least until the meet's over."

"Who? Everyone's practicing for the competition. I don't think it's fair to ask someone else to give up their time if I can't give up mine."

As Holly pulled into the rink's parking lot, she spied Kyle's rusty green car parked toward the rear of the building. "I'll figure something out," she said. "There's got to be a way." But she had no idea what it might be.

The girls hurried inside and quickly changed into their practice outfits. Holly was anxious to finish her warm-up so she would be ready to work with Steve when he arrived. She caught a glimpse of Kyle standing at the corner of the rink watching as she and Beth glided around the floor. As Holly came closer to him, Kyle beckoned to her with a wave of his hand. She noticed he wasn't wearing his skates.

"See you later," Holly said to Beth as she skated over to him. "Where are your skates?" she asked as cheerfully as possible.

He avoided her eyes, looking down at the floor. "I didn't think we'd be skating today. I heard the good news about you and Steve. Congratulations."

"Thanks, but what's that got to do with us?"

Kyle raised his head and gazed directly into Holly's eyes. "I appreciate your offer to work with me on my skating technique, but I know you've got a hard routine to learn and only four weeks to put it together. I don't want you sacrificing your chance for a trophy by wasting time with me."

"Thanks, Kyle, but my time wouldn't be wasted," she said quickly. "I'm sure we can work something out."

"Well, maybe if I were a competitive skater things would be different. . . ." His voice trailed off.

Then why don't you join the club and go for it? she wondered. She started to ask him, then stopped. It just wasn't the right time.

Holly gently put her hand on Kyle's arm. "Don't give up, Kyle. I really want to work with you. Somehow I'll make the time." She noticed Steve enter the rink and head for his locker. "I—I guess I better go now," she added with a shy smile.

As she started to leave, Kyle reached out and grabbed her hand. "Holly?"

"Yes?"

"I was wondering—would you go with me to the baseball game tomorrow night? Skating practice is over at five, and the game doesn't start till seven. Coach Gibson said I could have the night off."

Holly was startled. She liked Kyle a lot, but she'd never thought about going out with him on a date. "I don't know," she murmured. "I have to be at the rink pretty early Saturday morning. . . ."

"I'll take you straight home when the game's over," he said quickly. "That's a promise."

Holly hesitated. She didn't date much during skating season. Six days a week of practice at the rink and her schoolwork kept her on a tight schedule. But Kyle was so nice. Maybe one baseball game wouldn't hurt.

"Okay," she said, smiling. "I'd love to!"

His hazel eyes lit up. "Give me your address—I'll pick you up at six-thirty."

Only after Holly told him where she lived did he let go of her hand.

Holly and Steve spent the next hour working on the dance routine Coach Gibson had choreographed. Steve was extremely patient with her, explaining and demonstrating the many intricate moves. They worked on the difficult parts, going over each section time after time. "I think you're going to do just fine," he told her.

"Thanks for the vote of confidence," Holly said, smiling. "I'm going to give it my very best shot."

When practice was over for the afternoon, Holly felt a thrill of excitement and pride. *I can do it,* she said to herself. *I really can! I feel like the luckiest girl in town!*

Chapter Four

"**M**om, have you seen my pale blue cotton sweater?" Holly shouted from the top of the stairs the following night.

"Look in the second drawer of your dresser," Mrs. Benson shouted back. "That's where it was the last time I saw it."

Holly dashed into her room. It was already ten minutes after six, and Kyle was due in twenty minutes.

Opening the dresser, she found the sweater tucked way in the back under a pile of other clothes. *How does Mom always know where everything is?* she wondered. Holly pulled it from its hiding place, shoving the drawer closed with one knee. Hurriedly she tugged the sweater over her head, then brushed her hair vigorously. After she tied it back into a ponytail with a matching blue ribbon, she dabbed on a small amount of peach-colored lipstick. Deciding that her pale lashes needed a little help, she touched them with dark brown mascara. The sweater made her eyes look even bluer, and the denim jeans fit snugly, emphasizing her long legs and narrow waist. Satisfied with her appearance, she glanced at the clock on the nightstand by her bed. "Five minutes to spare," she said triumphantly. Slipping on a light jacket, she scooped up her shoulder bag and bounded down the stairs to the family room.

Her father was watching television, and her little brother was sprawled on the floor playing with his fleet of miniature cars. Holly sat down on the edge of the couch.

"Going to the baseball game?" Mr. Benson asked.

Holly nodded.

"Be home by eleven," he reminded her.

"I will. I've got a lesson with Steve in the morning."

The doorbell rang. "That must be Kyle," Holly said. She hurried to the door, but Jeffrey got there first and yanked it open. Kyle stood on the doorstep, looking very handsome in a red-and-white-striped shirt and khaki-colored jeans.

"Are you my sister's new boyfriend?" Jeffrey asked, gazing up at him.

"Jeffrey, *really*!" Holly groaned. She could feel her cheeks turning as red as the stripes on Kyle's shirt.

Kyle smiled at the little boy. "No," he said. "Just a friend."

Holly quickly stepped in front of Jeffrey. "Come in for a minute," she said. "I'd like you to meet my parents." She gave her brother a dirty look that sent him scampering off. "Just ignore him," she told Kyle. "He can be a real nuisance sometimes."

Kyle grinned. "Tell me about it. I have a younger brother *and* sister to put up with."

Holly led the way to the family room where her mother had joined her father. After she had introduced Kyle to her parents, Holly and Kyle left and walked to his car. Holly slid into the seat, fumbling with the stiff buckle of the seat belt.

"Hope you don't mind riding in this old junker," Kyle said as he got in and started the engine.

Laughing, Holly said, "As long as it runs, I couldn't care less."

Kyle drove away from the curb and down

the street. "Want to listen to some music?" he asked.

Holly nodded. She suddenly couldn't think of a thing to say. Music might make her silence less obvious.

Kyle turned on the radio, flipping from station to station. "How's this?" he said, pausing at one of them. He leaned forward and turned up the volume, glancing at Holly with a smile. "My favorite song."

"Really? Mine, too," Holly said, pleased that they liked the same kind of music.

They listened to the song in silence. "So where did you go to school before you moved to Linville?" Holly asked when the song was over.

"Enid, Oklahoma,"

"Did you like it there?"

"It was okay." Kyle's tone was flat and noncommittal.

He sure doesn't enjoy talking about himself, Holly thought. *At this rate, it's going to be a very quiet evening!*

A few silent minutes later, they pulled into the school parking lot, got out of the car, and walked to the entrance of the athletic field. Holly waited while Kyle purchased their tickets.

"Want something to drink before we find a seat?" he asked after he handed their tickets to the attendant.

"I am kind of thirsty," Holly admitted.

"How about some popcorn to go with our drinks?" Kyle suggested. "You should always have popcorn at a baseball game."

"And peanuts and Cracker Jacks," Holly added.

"You want all three?" Kyle offered.

Giggling, Holly said, "No. I was just thinking about that song, 'Take Me Out to the Ball Game.' Popcorn will be just fine."

They headed for the bleachers, carrying their popcorn and sodas. "Up here!" somebody yelled. Holly looked up and spied Beth and Drew waving from the top row.

"Want to sit with them?" Holly asked, pointing to the couple.

"Okay by me," Kyle said. "But why are they way up there?"

"Beth claims she can see the game better if she sits up high," Holly told him as they began the climb. "Also, she figures she's less likely to be hit on the head with a foul ball!"

"I should have known Beth would have good reasons," Kyle said with a grin.

They were seated just in time to stand up again as the teams trotted onto the field and a deep voice announced over the loudspeaker, "Ladies and gentlemen, our national anthem." Then the game began, and Holly was soon caught up in the excitement, cheering the Linville Lions on to victory. Almost before she realized it, it was time for the seventh inning stretch.

"Beth and I are going to get a couple of hot dogs," Drew said. "You guys want us to bring you anything?"

"How about some more soda?" Kyle asked Holly. "That popcorn was awfully salty."

"Sounds good to me," Holly agreed.

Kyle gave Drew some money, and after Drew and Beth started down the steps, Kyle and Holly took their seats again. To Holly's surprise, Kyle put his arm around her. It felt nice, and she wondered if he'd had a steady girlfriend back in Oklahoma.

"Beth may see better from up here," Kyle said, "but I feel like I need a pair of binoculars. Maybe next time we can convince them to sit a little further down, and the time after that, a few rows closer . . ."

Holly giggled. "Yeah—by the time the season's over, we'll be sitting in the dugout with the team." Then she caught herself. *What am I saying?* she thought. *Kyle's certainly not going to ask me to go to every game with him. And even if he did, I wouldn't be able to. I have too much schoolwork and practicing to do. And then there's the meet coming up in only four weeks. If only I had more time . . .*

"You okay?" Kyle asked, glancing down at her. "You look kind of worried all of a sudden."

"I'm fine," Holly said. "I was just thinking about all I have to do to get ready for the meet."

"I guess it must be pretty scary." Kyle tightened his arm around her briefly. "But I'm sure you'll do great. You'll blow the judges away."

Holly gave him a grateful smile. "I just wish I had more time to prepare."

"Yeah, I know what you mean," Kyle said. "I remember once when—"

"We're back," Beth sang out as she and Drew returned to their seats. "Here are your sodas."

I wonder what Kyle was going to say, Holly thought. *Too bad Beth and Drew weren't a few minutes later.*

During the ninth inning, the Linville Lions scored another run, winning the game four to one. After the game Holly and Kyle, Beth and Drew inched their way down the steps with the rest of the crowd. "Holly, do you and Kyle want to come over to my house and watch a movie with us?" Beth asked.

"I'd love to," Holly said, "but I'd better not. I have to be at the rink early in the morning for my lesson with Steve."

"And I promised to bring Holly home right after the game," Kyle added.

"Okay then. See you tomorrow."

Beth and Drew walked off hand in hand, and Holly and Kyle headed in the opposite direction toward the parking lot. Once they were in the car Kyle turned to Holly. "I hope you had a good time tonight. I know I did."

"I sure did. I haven't been to a baseball game in ages. Thanks for asking me," she said, smiling.

"Thanks for coming. I really like sports, but it's not much fun going to a game by yourself, and I don't know many people yet. Being the new kid in school is kind of hard sometimes."

"I guess it must be. I never thought about it much," Holly admitted. "I've done a lot of traveling because of my skating, but I've lived in Linville all my life. Has your family moved around a lot?"

"We used to," Kyle answered. "Dad worked in the oil fields so we had to go where his work took us."

"But there aren't any oil fields around here," Holly said, puzzled.

An unreadable expression crossed Kyle's face. "I know. Dad doesn't do that kind of work anymore."

Kyle soon turned onto Holly's street and

pulled up in front of her house. But instead of getting out, he sat with his hands on the steering wheel looking straight ahead. "Holly, can I ask you something?"

"Sure," she said, smiling.

He turned toward her then. "Would it make you nervous if I watched you and Steve work on your routine tomorrow?"

Holly laughed. "If I haven't gotten used to people watching me skate by now, I'd better give up! When Steve and I get through practicing, why don't you and I plan to have a lesson of our own?"

"I'd like that," he said. "And now I'd better get you into the house."

They walked side by side to Holly's front porch. "Thanks for a great time, Holly," Kyle said, taking her hand. Then to her surprise he bent down and gave her a tender kiss on the lips. Before she could react, he quickly turned and strode back to his car.

Holly stood on the porch, a warm, glowing feeling inside her making her forget about the chill in the night air. She waved to Kyle as he drove away, then touched her mouth. She had been kissed before, but there was something different about this particular kiss. Was it the *way* he had kissed her, or was it Kyle himself that made it so special?

Chapter Five

Holly dipped her spoon into her cereal and took a very small bite. "Are you feeling all right?" Mrs. Benson asked, looking at the soggy flakes floating in Holly's bowl.

"I know what's the matter with her," Jeffrey piped up. "She's in love with that guy she went out with last night." He picked up his glass and took a swallow of milk, wiping his mouth on his sleeve.

"I am not!" Holly retorted, glaring at her younger brother. "I'm just a little uptight about my lesson with Steve this morning. He's awfully good—I'm not sure I can do justice to the routine Coach Gibson's teaching us."

Mrs. Benson patted Holly's hand. "You can only do your best, honey. No one expects anything more than that. If the coach didn't think you were talented enough to skate with Steve, he wouldn't have offered you the opportunity."

Holly grinned. "Thanks for the pep talk, Mom. I just hope you're right!" She got up from the table and gave her mother a hug. "Guess I should get going."

"I'd feel better if you ate something," Mrs. Benson said, as Holly slipped on her jacket.

"I've got a bag of peanuts in my purse," Holly answered. "Energy food. I'll eat them at the rink—I promise."

A few minutes later, Holly parked her car in front of the rink, gathered her things, and headed for the entrance. As she opened the door, she spotted Kyle's old clunker entering the parking lot. Remembering last night's kiss and feeling suddenly shy, she paused for a moment, then hurried down the aisle to her locker and took out her skates and practice outfit.

"I'd better eat those peanuts before I go on the floor," Holly said to herself.

"What are you mumbling about?" Kyle said with a grin as he walked toward her. "Do you talk to yourself often?"

Holly blushed. "Not a lot—just every now

and then." She held up the bag of peanuts. "I was just about to have my breakfast. Want some?"

"Peanuts for breakfast, huh?" He leaned against the locker next to Holly's. "You have some very interesting habits, you know that?"

Holly began to munch on the peanuts. They seemed to go down more easily than the cereal had. After a moment of awkward silence, she said, "I had a really good time last night."

"I did, too," Kyle replied. "I hope we can do it again soon."

"Guess it'll depend on how the routine goes," Holly said. "I mean, I'll have to practice harder than ever."

Kyle nodded. "I understand. I know how important your skating is to you."

Holly finished the last peanut, wadded up the plastic bag, and stuck it in her jeans pocket. "Don't forget we're going to have a lesson together later today," she said, hoping she wasn't being too pushy. What if he'd changed his mind?

Kyle smiled at her. "I'm looking forward to it. Well, I'd better start cleaning the rink so I'll be all done when you're ready."

Relieved, Holly hurried into the dressing room and changed into a bright red skating skirt and white top. She quickly laced up her skates and glided out onto the floor.

Holly warmed up quickly, doing a few simple spins and jumps before heading to the figure circles. She tried to concentrate on following the lines on the floor, but found herself constantly glancing at the clock on the wall.

A few more skaters drifted into the rink. *Steve should be here any minute now,* Holly thought. She could feel all her muscles tighten, and her mouth suddenly felt dry. She wasn't sure if it was from nerves, or from the peanuts.

After she had taken a long drink at the water fountain, Holly saw Steve enter the rink and her stomach did a flip-flop. She rolled back onto the floor and continued to do her figures while she waited for him to join her.

"How about warming up with me?" Steve asked a few minutes later. Holly stopped in the middle of the figure she was doing and looked up at his smiling face. He didn't look very scary. Then why did he make her so nervous?

"Sure." She hoped he didn't hear the quiver in her voice.

As they skated around the edge of the rink, Holly began to feel herself relax. "That's it—take it easy," Steve said. "You're going to do fine."

They spotted Coach Gibson motioning them to join him in the middle of the floor. Holly looked up at the wall clock again. It was time for their lesson to begin.

"Okay, kids," he said. "First, I want you to listen to the music we're going to use for the routine. Then we'll slowly go through the steps. After that, it's just a matter of smoothing out the rough spots."

He makes it sound so easy, Holly thought to herself as the music began to play.

The next thirty minutes went by in a flash, and Holly enjoyed every second. There were a number of areas that needed work, but all in all, things went surprisingly well.

"Excellent," Coach Gibson said when the half hour was up. "You're both doing great. Steve, you've done an outstanding job of showing Holly the routine. I know it's not easy breaking in a new partner on such short notice."

"Thanks, Coach," Steve said. "Holly picks up on things real fast. Who knows? We might just have a shot at one of those trophies."

Holly felt her heart swell with pride.

"That's good to hear," Coach Gibson said.

43

"Take a ten-minute break, then practice by yourselves for another hour. We'll have another lesson on Wednesday afternoon."

As he skated off, Holly crossed to a bench and sat down while Steve went to the water fountain.

"I saw some of your lesson," Beth said, coming over to her. "I thought it looked terrific. Valerie will absolutely die with envy when she hears how good you are!"

Holly shook her head. "I doubt that. I'm not *that* good, and she knows I'll only be skating with Steve until her ankle heals."

"Well, you sure are giving her something to think about. Maybe she'll start being more serious about practicing when she gets back."

"Speaking about getting serious, how about it, partner?" Drew said as he skated up to them.

"Oh, here we go again," Beth groaned. "I can feel another lecture coming on." Making a face, she took Drew's hand. "See you later, Holly."

Holly looked around the rink for Kyle, but though he had been watching while she skated with Steve, she didn't see him now.

For the next hour, Holly and Steve worked diligently on their routine.

"That's enough for one day," Steve said at

44

last, twirling Holly around in a circle. "I don't know about you, but I'm beat!"

"Me, too," Holly agreed. "And I'm dying of thirst!" She skated over to the water fountain.

"Those peanuts will do it to you every time."

Holly looked up, water dribbling down her chin, to see Kyle standing beside her.

Blushing, she took a swipe at her face. "Hi," she said. "Thought I'd take a break before we start our lesson."

"I've got a better idea," Kyle said. "How about taking a break for a burger and some fries? You must have worked up an appetite by now, and the snack bar doesn't open for another hour. I'll drive."

"Do you have time?"

"Yep. I'm free until the afternoon session."

"But you really shouldn't skate on a full stomach," Holly said.

"One hamburger and a small order of fries is *not* going to give me a full stomach," Kyle replied. "That's what I consider a light snack."

"Give me five minutes to change," Holly said, smiling. "Meet you by the entrance, okay?"

Holly blinked as they walked out into the bright sunlight. She took a deep breath, inhaling the fresh, warm air. "What a pretty day," she said happily. "Makes you realize that summer's not very far away."

They walked hand in hand to Kyle's car. As soon as she got in, Holly rolled the window down and let the breeze caress her face while Kyle drove to the Burger Bar.

When they walked inside, Holly and Kyle were greeted by a blast of noise. Some teenagers were gathered around the video games lining one wall, and weird sounds echoed from the screens, competing with the jukebox that was blaring a popular rock song.

"What looks good?" Kyle yelled to Holly over the noise.

Holly decided on a hamburger, fries, and a strawberry milk shake, and Kyle selected the same with a chocolate shake.

Holly covered her ears with her hands while Kyle gave their order to the man behind the counter. "Why don't we eat outside?" she shouted. "I can't hear myself think in here!"

"Good idea," Kyle said. "Go ahead and find us a place—I'll bring the food."

Holly hurried to the door that led to an outside patio, found an empty table, and sat down, savoring the quiet.

"You looked great on the floor today," a boy said. Holly glanced up and saw Craig Adams, Valerie's boyfriend, who worked behind the snack bar at the rink.

"Thanks, Craig," she said. "I didn't know you were watching."

"Well, I was," Craig said. "Valerie should be pleased that Coach Gibson found such a good partner for Steve."

"How's her ankle doing?"

"Okay, I guess. But it's really bugging her that she won't be able to skate for a while. We were watching television at her house last night, and she said she'd never play volleyball again."

"I know how she feels," Holly said. "I'd be miserable if something like that happened to me."

Craig looked at his watch. "Well, guess I better get to the rink and set things up for the afternoon session. Coach Gibson yells if the hot dogs aren't just right."

"Tell Valerie I said hi and to hang in there," Holly said.

"Will do." He gave her a wave as he left the patio.

"Was that Craig?" Kyle asked, setting a tray full of food on the table.

"Yes. I was asking him how Valerie's doing."

"And . . . ?"

"Well, he didn't come right out and say it, but I get the feeling, knowing Valerie, that she's really mad about the whole thing."

"Surely she's not mad at *you*," Kyle said, taking a bite of his hamburger.

Holly frowned. "Well, I don't think she's too pleased that I'm skating with her partner."

"I guess I understand that," Kyle said.

"What do you mean?" Holly asked, puzzled.

Kyle stuck a french fry into his ketchup. "Oh, nothing. Forget it."

"Come on. You must have meant something. Confess."

Kyle avoided her eyes. "I just meant I wish it were me instead of Steve you were skating with."

I wish it were, too, Holly thought. Maybe this was the time to ask him why he didn't compete. "Kyle—" She began, but a familiar giggle interrupted her. "Hi," Beth said. She and Drew were standing behind them. Drew had a sack of fried onion rings, and Beth was carrying two large plastic cups of root beer.

"We thought we recognized your car," Drew

48

said to Kyle. "Mind if we join you? We're through skating for today."

"No problem," Kyle said.

As her friends sat down, Holly thought, *I wonder if I'll ever find out what Kyle's big secret is!*

When they had finished their meal, Holly and Kyle returned to the rink. Holly changed back into her practice costume, and when she emerged from the dressing room, she found Kyle waiting for her. "Want to warm up a little?" she asked. "There aren't many people on the floor yet."

Kyle nodded and took her hand. They circled the floor several times until Kyle said, "I guess I'm ready."

"Okay. What would you like to work on?" Holly asked.

"How about my doubles for a start?" he said. "I'm pretty rusty on some of them."

Now Holly was sure he'd been a serious skater and probably a competitor at some time in the past. *You don't learn how to do double jumps overnight,* she thought. *It takes a lot of work and long hours of practice.*

They skated over to a corner of the rink. "If you're going to do doubles, you'll need lots of room to pick up speed," Holly said. "I'll watch, and if I think you need any pointers, I'll let you know."

"Okay," Kyle said as he headed for the middle of the floor. "I'll start with a double axle."

Holly was amazed. *A double axle?*

Kyle skated around the floor. When the timing was just right, all at once he was spinning in the air. With his back arched and his arms outstretched, he made a perfect landing in front of Holly.

"How was it?" he said breathlessly.

"Terrific! Where'd you learn to skate like that?" she asked before she could stop herself.

"Oh, around," he said vaguely.

Holly watched in amazement while he performed a series of jumps and spins.

Kyle had just finished when Coach Gibson walked out into the center of the rink and blew his whistle. "Time for the afternoon session," he said. "You'll have to call it quits for today. There's no practice tomorrow so I expect all skating club members to be rested and ready to roll Monday after school."

Holly and Kyle left the floor with the rest of the skaters. "Guess I better get ready for work," Kyle said. "Thanks for all your help."

Holly laughed. "You're welcome. But I really didn't do anything. You know how to do those jumps as well as I do!"

Kyle shrugged. "Just lucky today, I guess. See you Monday." He headed toward the skate rental counter.

Holly entered the dressing room. Suddenly an idea came to her. Maybe there was a way to find out about Kyle's past skating experience, even if he wouldn't talk about it. She had the rest of the weekend to check it out, and check it out she would!

Chapter Six

Holly hurried home, eager to begin her search.

"Hi, honey!" Mrs. Benson said as she came out of the kitchen. "Are you through with practice for the day?"

"Yes," Holly replied, "I'm all done. It went pretty well, too."

"Oh, good! Your father and Jeffrey are at the library, so this will be a perfect time for you and me to go to Karen's Fabric Shop. I thought we'd pick out the material for your new costume."

Holly really wanted to go right up to her room and look through her old national skating programs, to see if Kyle's name might be in one of them. But she appreciated the time and effort her mother put into making her beautiful skating outfits, and they were included as part of the overall judging. *I'll just have to wait until later,* she thought.

At the fabric shop, Holly found a dazzling print in various shades of green accented with swirls of white. She decided to wear it for her figure-skating costume. But her favorite was the fabric she selected for the costume she'd wear skating free dance with Steve. It was a bright, shimmering turquoise with strands of silver thread woven in.

"I'll talk to Beth's mom about the trim," Mrs. Benson said to Holly on their way back home. "I think a pattern of silver sequins down the front and back of the bodice would be pretty. It will accent the hint of silver in the dress."

"Can you call her tonight?" Holly asked excitedly.

"I can do better than that," her mother replied, smiling. "Beth's parents are coming over after supper to play cards, and Beth's coming, too. Maybe we can decide then."

Holly leaned over and gave her mother a kiss. "Oh, Mom, you're the greatest! I can hardly wait to see it finished!"

*　　*　　*

That evening as Holly helped clear the supper dishes, she started thinking about Kyle again. Knowing that Beth would be coming over that night, Holly wrestled with the question of including her friend in her detective work. But could Beth keep her mouth shut? She wasn't the best person in the world at keeping secrets, and Holly definitely wanted this kept just between the two of them.

When Holly finished loading the dishwasher, she decided to go upstairs and start her homework. "Send Beth up when she gets here, okay?" she asked her mother.

Holly entered her room and sat down at her desk, staring at the algebra book in front of her. She opened it to the assigned page and read the first problem several times, but all that flashed before her mind's eye was Kyle doing a perfect double axle. She slammed the book closed and got up from her chair. "I've got to see what I can find out," she said aloud.

Holly crossed to a small bookshelf and pulled out a stack of National Roller-Skating Association programs from previous years. She sat down on the floor and carefully began leafing through them, hoping to spot Kyle's name among the competitors. With skaters from all over the country competing in so many different events, she knew it would take a long time, if she found anything at all.

"Hey, what are you doing?"

Holly looked up to see Beth standing in the doorway. "Come on in," she said. "And close the door."

Beth did, then walked over to where Holly was sitting on the floor surrounded by skating programs. "Why are you looking at these old things?" she asked.

Holly lowered her voice. "Can you keep a secret?"

"Of course," Beth replied, and plopped down next to Holly. "About what?"

"No, I mean a *real* secret," Holly said. "You can't tell a soul, not even Drew. Promise?"

Beth solemnly raised her right hand. "I promise."

Holly took a deep breath. "Okay. You didn't come back to the rink after lunch today, did you?"

"No. I had to baby-sit for Mrs. Foster."

"Well," Holly said, "after lunch Kyle and I went back to the rink so I could help him with his skating technique."

"And . . . ?" Beth said, leaning forward.

"The first thing he did was a double axle!"

"A *what*?" Beth said, her eyes widening.

"A double axle, and he landed perfectly."

Beth shook her head. "That's hard to believe. An axle is one of the hardest jumps to do."

"I know," Holly said, "but it's true. And a double is even harder. He also did a lot of other really difficult jumps and spins. After that, I decided he *must* have competed before, but he won't admit it."

"So you thought you'd go through these old programs and see if you could find his name, right?"

"Right," Holly said.

Beth whistled. "Wow. I feel just like Nancy Drew!" She picked up a program and started flipping through the pages.

"Go through all the events Kyle could have possibly skated in while I search through this one," Holly said.

The room was silent except for the rustle of pages being turned. Beth finished looking through her program and said, "Nothing incriminating in that one."

"Incriminating?" Holly echoed. "Aren't you getting a little carried away with playing detective?"

"I'm just trying to get in the right mood," Beth teased. "Give me another one."

Holly gave a second program to Beth and finished paging through her own. "Nothing in this one either."

"Maybe he didn't go to Nationals," Beth said. "A lot of skaters don't. You can only go if you place at the regional level."

"I know," Holly replied. "It's a long shot, but at least it's a starting place."

"Why don't you just ask him? It'd be a lot easier than going through all these programs."

"I've tried. But every time I do, he changes the subject. It's like he doesn't want to talk about it. I don't know. Maybe I should just leave it alone. It's really none of my business anyway."

"Well, now that we've started we might as well finish," Beth pointed out.

They continued to search the programs until Holly suddenly shouted, "Here it is!" She pointed to Kyle's name halfway down the page.

Beth leaned closer. "Where? Where?"

"Right here. Look! Kyle Evans." Holly placed her finger on Kyle's name. "And look at the date on the cover," she said. "This was two years ago."

"Hmmm . . . I wonder what that means?" Beth mused.

"I don't know," Holly answered. "Let's check through the programs for the last two years again and make sure we didn't miss his name."

They carefully scanned the pages of the earlier programs, but Kyle was not listed.

"Maybe his name was left out when the programs were printed," Beth suggested.

"Possibly," Holly said. "But it'd be strange for something like that to happen two years in a row. That's why I don't think he skated at Nationals for the last two years." She frowned. "Now the question is, why?"

"Good luck," Beth said dryly. "If Kyle's as closemouthed about it as you say, you may never find out."

"Come on, Beth. We're going to be *so* late," Holly said on Monday afternoon. She grabbed her purse and skating bag from the backseat of her car and slammed the door shut.

"I'm coming!" Beth slung her purse over her shoulder. "Of all times for my lock to jam! I thought the custodian was never going to get my locker opened."

Holly noticed Steve's car in the parking lot. "Oh, boy—Steve's already here. I hope he hasn't been waiting too long."

"I'm really sorry," Beth said.

"Forget it," Holly replied. "It wasn't your fault."

The girls walked quickly into the rink and down the aisle to their lockers. Holly set her skating bag on the floor, pulling out a yellow practice outfit and a pair of clean socks. Then she dialed her combination and opened her locker. As she took out her skates, she moaned, "Oh, no!"

"What's the matter?" Beth asked.

Holly held up her skates. "Look."

"Where are your laces?"

"That's what I'd like to know. I don't remember taking them out on Saturday." She pawed through her locker, but there were no laces.

Beth frowned. "Are you sure you didn't take them home to wash when you took all your other stuff?"

"I'm *pretty* sure," Holly said. "And I don't have a spare pair with me."

"Here—I've got some extras." Beth took a pair from the shelf of her locker and handed them to Holly.

"Thanks, Beth. You're a lifesaver!" Holly sat down on the floor and began threading a lace through the eyelets of one skate while Beth picked up the other skate and did the same. It took a long time, and by the time the girls had changed and skated out onto the floor, Holly was fifteen minutes late for her lesson with Steve. "Maybe I should forget my warm-up," she murmured. "Surely one time won't hurt." She skated over to where Steve was practicing his figures, saying breathlessly, "Sorry I'm late!"

"That's okay. I needed to work on some stuff anyway. Have you warmed up?"

Holly looked at the floor. "Uh—no, not really."

"Then you'd better take a couple of laps," he said. "You don't want any pulled muscles."

"Okay. I guess you're right."

As Holly skated around the floor, she saw Kyle standing by the railing, leaning on a push broom. She smiled and waved, and he waved back. Holly hadn't spoken to him since she'd found his name in the program. She was eager to ask him about it, but there hadn't been an opportunity. *Maybe later today,* she thought.

Holly glided around the rink, taking long strokes, forcing her leg muscles to relax, and Beth skated beside her. Glancing down at her feet, Holly said, "I wonder where my laces disappeared to?"

"Maybe somebody needed to borrow a pair and hasn't returned them yet," Beth suggested.

"But no one knows the combination to my locker except you and me." Holly shook her head. "Weird. Well, I guess right now I'd better concentrate on practicing with Steve." She skated over to him. "All set."

"Good." He took her hand. "Let's go."

As the minutes passed, Holly forgot about the missing skate laces, giving her full attention to the routine she and Steve would perform in three weeks.

"That was pretty good," Steve said when they had finished the dance. "Let's take a break."

"Okay," Holly agreed. "I could use a breather."

As they left the floor and sat down on a bench near the snack bar, Craig walked by carrying a box of candy bars.

"Hi, Craig," Holly said.

"Looks like you're working hard," Steve added.

Craig didn't respond. He just entered the snack bar and slammed the box down on the counter.

Holly looked at Steve. "Wonder what's bugging him?"

"Valerie's probably taking it out on him because she can't skate," Steve said. "She can be a real pain sometimes. She's a good dance partner, but I'm sure glad she's not my girlfriend." He stood up. "Come on. Break's over. Let's go practice some more."

Holly and Steve continued to work for another hour until Coach Gibson blew the whistle signaling that practice was over for the day.

Holly and Steve skated off the floor. "You're coming along fine," Steve said. "See you tomorrow."

As he headed for his locker, Kyle came over to Holly.

"Hi," he said, smiling.

Holly felt her heart beat a little faster. "Hi."

"Your routine's looking better every day."

"Thanks. Steve's been a big help." She smiled. "Sorry I didn't get to skate with you today."

"Me, too."

"Maybe there'll be time tomorrow," Holly said.

"Maybe," Kyle replied, but he didn't sound too hopeful. "Got time for a soda before you go home?"

Holly hesitated. "I better not. I've got to study for a chemistry test and do some algebra problems."

"Oh, come on. One little soda?"

Holly shook her head slowly. "No, Kyle, I really can't. Coach Gibson doesn't let anyone compete who doesn't keep their grades up."

"Okay. Tomorrow then." Kyle turned away abruptly and walked off.

Great. Now he's mad at me, Holly thought as she entered the dressing room. Most of the other skaters had already left, but Beth was waiting for her. "Where've you been?" she asked.

"I was talking to Kyle."

"Oh?" Beth fluttered her lashes.

"No, not *that* kind of talk." Holly changed her clothes quickly and picked up her skates. Beth followed her to the lockers, where they put their things away, got their purses, and walked outside.

The sky had turned cloudy, blotting out the sun, and the wind whipped at their coats, warning of an impending storm. Holly looked up into the darkening sky. "Looks like it's going to rain. Let's hurry."

They got into the car, and Holly pulled out onto the street. Beth turned toward her. "Well?"

"Well what?"

"Well, when are you going to talk to Kyle about his name being in that program?"

Holly drummed her fingers on the steering wheel as she waited for the light to turn green. "I don't know. It has to be the right time."

"When will that be?" Beth asked. "I need my beauty sleep, and I don't sleep well when

I'm in the midst of a mystery—make that *two* mysteries."

"What do you mean?"

"Your skate laces. What happened to them?"

Holly shrugged. "That may be one mystery we'll never solve."

As she sat at her desk later that night, Holly thought about what Beth had said earlier. *She's right,* Holly thought. *There are two mysteries. Kyle's reluctance to talk about his past is one; and where in the world did my skate laces disappear to?*

Chapter Seven

The next morning when Holly woke up, the sunlight was streaming through her window. The previous evening's storm had disappeared, leaving a clean, fresh scent in the air.

She hummed to herself as she got ready for school. With the promise of a beautiful day, yesterday's mystery of the missing skate laces was forgotten.

"Morning, everybody," Holly said as she entered the kitchen. "What smells so good?"

"Pancakes," Jeffrey told her. "My favorite."

"Mine, too," Holly said. She helped herself to two large pancakes and a piece of sausage.

"I'm glad you're eating so well today," her mother said. "I was concerned about how little you ate for supper last night."

"I guess I was kind of tired. But I'm really hungry this morning. Besides, you make the best pancakes in the world."

"You're not overdoing it at the rink, are you, honey?" her father asked. "Keeping up with your schoolwork and going to skating practice every day is quite a responsibility."

Holly smiled. "I know, Dad. But really, I'm fine. You know how much I love to skate, and I haven't gotten anything below a *B* all semester."

"By the way," Mr. Benson said, "before I forget, next Sunday is Linville's Annual Spring Festival and Picnic. Does everybody want to go?"

"Yes!" Jeffrey shouted. "Are they gonna have pony rides again this year?"

"I think so," Mr. Benson replied. "And a Moon Walk, too." He turned to Holly. "Beth is welcome to come with us if you want to invite her."

"Thanks, Dad," Holly said. "I'll ask her today."

Mrs. Benson glanced at the kitchen clock. "Look at the time! You all had better get moving."

Holly ran into the hall, and picked up her backpack and purse. "I'll be home after practice," she called over her shoulder as she ran out the door.

Beth was waiting at the curb in front of her house when Holly drove up. "You're almost late," she accused, sliding into the front seat.

"If I'm *almost* late," Holly said cheerfully, "then I must be on time. Dad was talking about the Spring Festival at breakfast, and I lost track of the time. It's next Sunday. Want to go with us?"

"Next Sunday? I can't. We're going to Oak Grove to have dinner with Aunt Martha. Mom's already made plans." Beth gave Holly a sly glance. "Maybe you could ask Kyle?"

"Hmmm—I hadn't thought of that," Holly said. "But after what happened at the rink yesterday afternoon, I'm not sure he'd go. He was pretty ticked off because I couldn't stay and have a soda with him."

The warning bell rang as Beth and Holly hurried up the steps to the school entrance. "See you at lunch," Beth shouted over the roar of voices as the students piled into the building.

Holly ran down the hall to her locker. She

was taking out her books when somebody tapped her on the shoulder. She turned around.

"Hi, Holly," Kyle said. He looked uncomfortable. "Look, I want to apologize for the way I acted yesterday afternoon at the rink. You must think I'm a real jerk."

Holly smiled. "No, I don't. I wanted to stay, but I was really swamped with homework." The final bell rang. "Uh-oh—we'd better get to homeroom."

"Right. See you later." He took her hand and gently squeezed it, then walked off down the hallway.

He's not mad anymore, Holly thought happily. *Maybe I'll ask him to the festival after all!*

At lunchtime, Holly hurried to the pay phone next to the school office and called her mother to find out if she could invite Kyle.

"Is he the boy you went to the baseball game with the other night?" Mrs. Benson asked.

"Yes," Holly said.

"I don't see why not. He seemed like a nice boy. I'm sure it would be all right with your father."

"Thanks, Mom! I gotta go. 'Bye."

Holly hung up the phone and headed for the

cafeteria. "Mom said I could ask him," she told Beth as they carried their trays to a table.

"Your mom said you could ask who what?"

"I can ask Kyle to the festival!" Holly said.

"Think he'll accept your offer?"

Holly grinned. "I'm pretty sure he will."

"You weren't so sure this morning," Beth reminded her.

"We made up," Holly said. "I'm going to ask him as soon as we get to the rink this afternoon."

The rest of the day seemed to take forever, but at last, Holly and Beth were on their way to practice.

"What's the rush?" Beth asked as Holly raced inside. "You've got all afternoon to ask him."

"I want to do it before I start practice," Holly said.

"You're really excited about this, aren't you?"

Holly grinned sheepishly. "Does it show that much?" she asked.

"Uh-huh. Maybe you should play it down. You know, act nonchalant. Be cool."

Holly thought for a minute. "You might be right. I'll try it."

"Try what?" Kyle said, walking up to the two girls.

The words popped out of Holly's mouth before she could stop them. "Would you like to come to the Linville Spring Festival with me and my family on Sunday?" she asked all in a rush.

"Whoa, slow down!" Kyle said, laughing. "Would I like to *what*?"

Holly took a deep breath. "Linville's having its annual spring festival this coming Sunday. I—I was wondering if you'd like to go with me. And my family," she added quickly.

"Sounds like fun," Kyle said, "but I'll have to check with my parents. I'll call you tonight and let you know for sure, okay?"

"Okay!" Holly said, elated. "Well, I guess I'd better go change. . . ."

Beth rolled her eyes. "That was *really* subtle," she said as she and Holly went into the dressing room.

"Do you think I came on too strong?" Holly asked anxiously.

Beth giggled. "Put it this way—playing it cool is definitely *not* one of your talents. But he certainly didn't seem to mind. That guy likes you a whole lot."

Holly blushed. "You really think so?"

"I really think so. Now take your right skate off your left foot," Beth said, "or else you're going to fall flat on your face!"

*   *   *

Later that night, Holly sat at her desk staring at her history book and waiting for the phone to ring. *Come on, Kyle,* she urged silently. *I'm sure I'll have a much better understanding of the Revolutionary War after you call.*

She had almost given up hope when the telephone finally rang. "I'll get it!" Holly shouted, lunging for the receiver of the phone on her desk. "Hello?" she said, as casually as she could.

"Holly? This is Kyle."

Play it cool, she told herself.

"Oh, hi, Kyle. How are you?"

"Fine. Sorry I couldn't call you earlier. I had to wait for my mother to get home from work."

"Oh, that's okay. I've been buried in my homework all night," Holly said, glancing at the pile of unopened textbooks in front of her.

"I asked my parents about Sunday," he went on, "and they said I can go as long as I get my chores done."

Forgetting to be cool, Holly cried, "Great! Why don't you plan to be at my house around ten-thirty Sunday morning?"

"Sounds good to me." He paused. "Will you be at the rink tomorrow?"

"Sure. I have another lesson with Steve."

"Okay. See you then."

She hung up the phone and picked up her history book, a triumphant smile on her face.

Chapter Eight

Holly was even more eager than usual to get to the rink on Wednesday afternoon. But when she and Beth got into her car and Holly turned the key in the ignition, nothing happened.

She turned the key again. Still nothing. "Great. Now what's the matter?" Holly said, exasperated. "I just took this thing to the shop a couple of weeks ago!"

"Maybe you're out of gas," Beth suggested.

"No way. I filled the tank before I picked you up this morning."

Beth frowned. "Well, what do we do now?"

"I don't know," Holly said. "But whatever

it is, we have to do it fast. I can't be late *again* for my lesson with Steve."

She turned the key one more time, but the car still refused to start. She sighed. "I guess I'd better go back inside and call Mom." Holly got out of the car, and Beth followed her.

They were on their way up the school steps when they met Kyle coming down. "Hi— what's happening?" he said.

"Problems," Holly told him. "My car won't start, and I've got a lesson at the rink in a few minutes. I was just going to call my mother and ask her to pick me up."

"Want me to take a look?" Kyle asked. "If it's something minor, maybe I can fix it for you."

Holly heaved a sigh of relief. "That would be great!"

When they reached the car, Kyle opened the hood and peered inside.

"See anything wrong?" Holly asked.

"Not yet. Got a flashlight?"

Beth found one in the glove compartment, and Holly turned it on, moving the beam as Kyle directed.

"Ah-ha!" he exclaimed. "I think I found your problem. The coil wire from the distributor cap is loose on one end. Got a screwdriver handy?"

"I keep a toolbox in my trunk." After Holly

found the screwdriver, she held the flashlight while he did something mysterious to the coil.

"All done," he said a moment later.

"Thanks so much!" Holly said.

"Nothing to it." Then Kyle frowned. "It's kind of puzzling, though. . . ."

"What is?"

"Well, I can't figure out how that wire got loose."

"Really?" Holly said. "Is it unusual for that to happen?"

"Yeah. Well, it should be okay now. Why don't I get in and see if it starts?"

He turned the key in the ignition, and the motor began to purr.

"You're a genius!" Holly exclaimed.

"Of course," Kyle said smugly, getting out of the car. "Was there ever any doubt?"

Laughing, Holly said, "Thanks again." Standing on tiptoe, she gave him a quick kiss on the cheek.

"See you at the rink," Kyle said, and waved, heading for his own car.

As Holly drove out of the parking lot, Beth teased, "Do you always kiss your auto mechanic?"

Holly grinned. "Only on very special occasions. Thanks to Kyle, I shouldn't be more than fifteen minutes late for my lesson."

Steve was a little annoyed when Holly showed up late, but in spite of that, their lesson went well.

"How are your dresses for the meet coming?" Beth asked the next afternoon as the girls headed for their lockers at the rink.

"Oh, fine. Mom's almost got my figure dress finished, and she said she was going to work on my dance dress tomorrow," Holly said, starting to twist the dial on her lock. She looked at it with a puzzled expression.

"What's the matter?" Beth asked.

"I'm not sure. My lock is stiff."

"Maybe you need to spray some oil on it."

"Maybe." Holly finished dialing her combination, but when she pulled down on the lock it didn't open. "That's strange," she muttered, and tried it again with the same results.

"Here—let me try." Beth carefully turned the dial to the proper numbers but nothing happened.

Now Holly took hold of the lock and looked at it closely. "*That's* the problem!" she exclaimed.

"What?" Beth asked.

"This isn't my lock. Someone's put another lock on my locker!"

"That's crazy," Beth said. "Why would any-one do that?"

"Why would anyone take my skate laces?" Holly replied, frowning.

"Uh-oh, guess who's headed this way," Beth murmured, as Steve skated up to the girls, pointedly looking at his watch.

"What's the matter now?" he asked irritably.

"Someone put a different lock on my locker," Holly told him. "I can't open it."

"Well, get it off somehow," Steve snapped. "We need to practice, you know. I'll be on the floor whenever you're ready." He turned and skated away.

"Boy, he sure is edgy today," Beth said. "What's his problem, anyway?"

"Probably me," Holly replied with a sigh. "I guess I'd better find Coach Gibson. He'll know what to do."

"I'll go with you," Beth offered.

"No, you go on and practice. No reason for both of us to get in trouble."

Beth took her things out of her locker and started toward the dressing room just as Kyle came down the hall.

"Hi, Holly," he said. "How's it going?"

Holly made a face. "Not great. I guess it just isn't my day."

"What do you mean?"

"I can't open my locker—somebody switched locks on me," Holly said. "On top of that, Steve's kind of upset with me. I was just about to look for Coach Gibson to see if he can help me get the lock off."

"He left the rink a few minutes ago to run an errand," Kyle told her. "Let me see what I can do. I'm pretty sure there's a crowbar in the storage room. Be right back."

He hurried off and returned with the crowbar a few minutes later. He ran it through the lock, twisted it with all his strength, and it snapped in two. "There," Kyle said, stepping back. "You're all set."

"Thanks," Holly said. "You're a lifesaver!"

He grinned at her. "Yesterday I got a kiss for fixing your car. Do I get one for breaking into your locker, too?"

Laughing, Holly lightly kissed his cheek. "I'd better get my stuff and change. Thanks again."

"Anytime," Kyle said.

Holly quickly changed into her practice clothes and skated onto the floor. "I'm sorry," she said, gliding over to Steve.

"Sorry won't cut it," he said sharply. "This is the second time in two days you've been late. I'm not going to skate with somebody who isn't responsible enough to show up on time!"

Holly could feel tears well up in her eyes. "Steve, that's not fair! I *am* responsible. But sometimes things just happen that a person doesn't have any control over."

"Well, you better *get* control," Steve muttered. "If it happens again, I'm going to ask Coach Gibson to find me another partner. Come on—let's see if you can remember the routine."

Holly tried her best to give her full attention to her skating but everything she attempted was a disaster. "I don't know what's the matter with me," she moaned when Steve helped her up off the floor after she'd fallen for the third time.

"We might as well give up for today," he said. "We're getting nowhere fast."

Holly sighed. "Maybe you're right. Things will be better tomorrow, honest."

"They'd better be," Steve said in disgust as he skated off.

Holly skated over to the figure circles. *Maybe I can concentrate on these,* she thought, but her skates kept wobbling and went outside the line. Discouraged, she left the floor and sat down on a bench near the dressing rooms, staring glumly at her feet.

A moment later, Kyle sat down next to her and took her hand. "It can't be that bad," he said softly.

Holly looked at him. "I can't seem to do anything right today," she said, her voice trembling.

"Hey, we all have days like that," Kyle said. "Nobody's perfect all the time, not even me."

Holly gave him a faint smile. "Thanks for trying to cheer me up." They stood. "Guess I might as well get dressed and wait for Beth."

"If there's anything I can do, just let me know," Kyle said.

Holly squeezed his hand. "Thanks, Kyle. You're a real friend." He released her hand, and she skated off to the dressing room.

"How did your lesson go today?" Beth asked a short while later as she and Holly walked to the car.

"Awful," Holly told her. "Steve was mad because I was late again. He threatened to ask Coach Gibson for another partner if I don't start showing up on time. And then when we started to practice, I just kept fouling up. Steve was really steamed."

Beth shook her head. "Wow. No wonder you look so down. But I wouldn't worry about Steve finding another partner. Nobody else could learn your part in such a short time—there's only a little over two weeks before the meet."

"Don't remind me!" Holly said with a shudder. "The way things are going, I'll *never* get this routine down in time!"

Holly dropped Beth off at her house and drove home in a somber mood. At her own house, she found a note lying on the table by the stairs.

> Honey,
>   Your father and I are out shopping and Jeffrey is at the baby-sitter's. There's a platter of cold chicken and potato salad in the fridge. Have all you want.
>   Love,
>   Mom

Holly walked into the kitchen, opened the refrigerator door, and picked up a chicken leg. But after one bite, she wrapped it up and put it back. "I'm just not hungry," Holly said aloud. "Might as well do my homework."

She attempted to muddle her way through her assignments, but she had a hard time focusing on her work. The events of the past few days kept flashing in her mind—the missing laces, the problem with the car, and now the lock.

What was going on, anyway? Was somebody playing practical jokes on her, or did someone want to cause her real problems? And if so, who?

Could it possibly be Valerie? Holly wondered, then shook her head. No way. Valerie might resent Holly's skating with Steve, but she hadn't been to the rink since she broke her ankle. Who else might have a grudge against her? Holly couldn't think of anyone.

She began pacing the floor. *I can't let anything interfere with this meet,* Holly thought. *Even when I get another lock, maybe I'd better put my things in Beth's locker for a while. I'm sure she wouldn't mind.*

Holly went over to the phone on her nightstand and dialed Beth's number. When Beth picked up the phone, she said, "Listen, Beth, I've got a favor to ask of you. Could I put my skating stuff in your locker at the rink for a while, until the meet's over?"

"Of course, but why?"

"Well, I don't want anything more to happen that might ruin my chances of skating with Steve. It's too important to me."

"Do you think somebody's trying to prevent you from dancing with him?" Beth asked, sounding amazed.

"I don't know," Holly confessed. "I guess it sounds crazy, but it seems like sabotage to me."

"Why don't you tell Coach Gibson or your parents about it?" Beth suggested.

Holly sighed. "I can't do that. I don't have any proof—just this weird feeling. Please don't say anything to anyone about this," she added. "I want to keep it as quiet as possible."

"Right," Beth said. "I understand. You can count on me."

The baffling incidents that had been plaguing Holly suddenly seemed to stop. Her confidence in her skating returned, and Steve's attitude changed to one of encouragement and praise.

Coach Gibson beamed as he watched the pair go through their routine on Saturday morning.

"I'm very proud of you both," he said when they had finished. "You've been working extremely hard, and it shows. Over the next two weeks, we'll concentrate on smoothing out one or two rough spots, but even now, you guys look terrific."

Steve took Holly's hand. "Let's get a little more practice in before I have to go to work, okay? We need to coordinate that last sit-spin better."

"That's the spirit," Coach Gibson said.

As they glided around the floor rehearsing their routine, Holly was aware of Kyle watching her every move, and once again she wished that he were her partner. Would she and Kyle ever have a chance to skate together?

Chapter Nine

A burst of bright May sunshine came through Holly's bedroom window as she twirled in front of the mirror on Sunday morning. She eyed her reflection critically, studying the outfit she'd chosen to wear for the Spring Festival—a navy blue split skirt and a short-sleeved blue-and-white-striped shirt. *I hope Kyle likes it,* she thought, and checked her makeup one more time before she went downstairs to the kitchen.

"My, you look nice," Holly's mother said, handing her a big paper bag full of things for the picnic. "Would you take these out to the car for me?"

"Sure," Holly replied.

She carried the bag out to where her father was loading the car with other picnic gear. Mr. Benson moved a folding chair to another spot in the crowded trunk to make room for it. "I hope there's room for us in the car," he said, laughing. "Your mother has enough stuff here for *three* picnics!" He and Holly both looked up as they heard the squeaks and groans of Kyle's ancient car coming down the street. "What's that racket?" her father asked.

Holly giggled. "Kyle's car," she said. "Noisy, isn't it?"

"Sure is," Mr. Benson agreed.

Holly waved to Kyle as he pulled over to the curb. He got out of his car and walked up the driveway, carrying a tray of delicious-looking brownies. He was wearing neatly pressed chinos and a dark green polo shirt. "Mom wanted to contribute something to the picnic," he said. "I hope these will be okay."

Mr. Benson smiled. "How nice of her. They look great." He took the tray and put the brownies into a large cooler in the trunk.

"Whoa, Paint!" Jeffrey hollered, bounding around the corner of the house. He was wearing cowboy boots and a bright red cowboy hat.

"Who's Paint?" Kyle asked, grinning at the little boy.

"My horse," Jeffrey said. "He's make-believe, but I'm going to ride *real* ponies today."

"Oh, I see," Kyle said and winked at Holly.

Mr. Benson started for the house. "I'd better find out what's keeping your mother. You two keep an eye on Jeffrey and that wild stallion of his."

"No problem," Kyle said. "I love horses."

"Really?" Jeffrey asked. "Do you have a horse?"

"I used to a long time ago, when we lived in Texas."

"Really?" Holly echoed.

"Yeah—I used to ride a lot."

"Cool!" Jeffrey exclaimed.

Just then Mr. and Mrs. Benson came out of the house. "I *know* we forgot something," Mrs. Benson was saying.

"Impossible," Mr. Benson said. "The car's so full that there's barely room for all five of us."

"Holly and I can go in my car," Kyle offered. "It's a clunker, but it runs."

Mr. Benson looked at him thoughtfully. "That might not be a bad idea. You never know what extra junk we might end up dragging home with us from the festival."

"Maybe we could bring home a pony!" Jeffrey cried.

"That is a definite no," his father replied. "Don't even *think* about it. Understood?"

"Okay," Jeffrey said a little sadly.

"We'll follow you," Kyle said.

He and Holly walked down the driveway and got into his car. "I haven't had a chance to tell you how nice you look," Kyle said as Holly buckled her seat belt.

"Thanks," Holly said. She knew she was blushing. "You look nice, too."

Kyle put the car into gear and followed Mr. Benson down the winding street. Then he turned on the radio.

Holly settled back in her seat, smiling. "That's my favorite station," she said.

Kyle grinned. "It's mine, too. I really like country-western music."

"It's the best," Holly agreed. "Who's your favorite singer?"

For the rest of the drive, they talked about music. The trip didn't seem long at all. When they arrived at the picnic grounds, everyone filled their arms with picnic paraphernalia.

They made their way to an empty picnic table under a large maple tree. While Mr. Benson and Kyle set up the chairs, Holly and her mother spread a green-and-white-checkered cloth on the table. Then her father and Kyle set the cooler and the various bulging bags on top of it as Jeffrey hopped from one foot to the other, waiting impatiently for everyone to finish.

Mr. Benson looked at his watch. "It's half past eleven. We'll have lunch in about an hour, but first let's check out the rides and try our skill at some of the games."

"Look—there's a Ferris wheel, and a carousel, and bumper cars," Holly said, pointing to the amusement area.

"Where are the ponies?" Jeffrey yelled.

"Why don't we go see?" Mr. Benson said, and Jeffrey shot across the park as his mother and father followed more slowly.

"What would you like to do first?" Holly asked Kyle.

"It all looks like fun," he replied. "How about the bumper cars?"

They crossed over to the bumper cars and took their place at the end of a long line of people waiting to buy tickets. Holly saw several kids she knew from school, and they waved at each other.

"There are sure a lot of people here," Kyle said, looking around. "Is there always such a big crowd at these things?"

"Oh, yes," Holly said. "The Spring Festival is one of Linville's biggest events. Everybody in town comes."

After the bumper cars, Holly and Kyle went on several other rides, some of them twice.

"How about trying our luck at some of the games?" Kyle said when they got off the Ferris wheel. "Maybe I can win you a purple teddy bear!"

Holly laughed. "I've always wanted a purple teddy bear!"

They strolled over to a row of booths where several types of games were set up. Kyle stood back a minute studying them. "Think I'll try this one," he said at last. "It doesn't look too hard. All you have to do is try to break three balloons with those darts. If you break all three, you win a prize."

He gave the attendant some money, and the man gave him three darts. Kyle took careful aim, and the first dart popped an orange balloon with a loud bang. His second dart exploded a yellow balloon. Grinning at Holly, he said, "Only one more to go."

She held her breath as Kyle threw the last dart—and popped a third balloon.

"Hurray!" Holly shouted, clapping her hands.

"Well, what prize would you like?" Kyle asked.

Holly cocked her head to the side and peered at the array of stuffed animals displayed on the shelves. "Hmmm—no purple teddy bears. In that case, I think I'd like the neon-pink giraffe."

The attendant took a small stuffed giraffe from the shelf and handed it to Holly. "All yours, little lady. Your boyfriend's got some pitching arm there."

Holly blushed.

"Thanks," Kyle said.

As they walked away from the booth, Holly looked shyly at Kyle. "I've never had anybody win something for me before." Then she had an idea. "I'll take it to the meet with me! It's a tradition to take your favorite stuffed animal to a meet for your coach to hold while you're competing. It's supposed to bring you good luck."

"You don't need luck," Kyle said. "You've got skill. You're a top-notch skater."

Holly smiled. "Thanks, Kyle. I just hope you're right."

"Bet you a strawberry milk shake you come home with a trophy."

Laughing, Holly said. "I love milk shakes! I promise to do my best."

"My stomach tells me it's time for lunch." Kyle looked at his watch. "What do you know? My stomach's right."

"Then let's go!" Holly said.

Chapter Ten

"I haven't eaten this much in ages," Kyle said to Holly, leaning back in his folding chair. "Your mother gets an *A*-plus for her cooking skills."

"Your mom does, too," Holly said. "Those brownies were fantastic." She stood up and stretched. "What would you like to do now?"

Kyle groaned. "Just sit here. I feel like I'm going to explode any minute."

"Well, we can't have that." Holly grabbed Kyle by the hand, pulling him to his feet. "Come on. Let's walk over to the lake and feed the ducks."

"Please!" Kyle moaned. "Don't mention

food to me for at least another hour. Where is this lake?"

"Just on the other side of that hill." Holly pointed in the opposite direction from where the rides were located. She took a few slices of bread from a plastic bag lying on the picnic table. "Okay if Kyle and I go feed the ducks?" she asked her parents.

"Sure, dear," Mr. Benson said.

Holly glanced at Kyle, who was staring at the hill as if it were Mount Everest. "Think you can make it?" she teased.

"If you can, I can," he said, and took her hand.

They soon reached the top. "Isn't it beautiful?" Holly said, pointing to the sparkling blue water shimmering below them.

Kyle gazed at the view, obviously impressed. "I didn't realize there were such scenic places in the Midwest. I thought it was nothing but corn and wheat fields."

Still hand in hand, they walked in silence to the lake. A few people were strolling around the banks, watching the graceful movements of the swans and feeding the ducks.

Holly handed Kyle a couple of slices of bread, and they tore them into small pieces and tossed them into the water, attracting ducks from all over the lake.

"Too bad these guys couldn't have joined

us for lunch," Kyle said. "Then your mom wouldn't have so many leftovers." He threw his last piece into the water.

"That's all, fellas," Holly said. "How about a walk around the lake?" she suggested to Kyle. "There's a pretty little cove not far from here—it's my favorite spot."

They strolled slowly along the bank until they reached the cove. Holly sat down on the grass near the edge of the lake, dipping her fingers in the cool water. "It's so peaceful," she murmured almost to herself. "When I come here, I forget all about my problems and just dream."

Kyle sat down next to her. "You're the last person I'd expect to have any problems. You always seem so cheerful and confident."

"Not always," Holly replied. "There are times when I get kind of depressed and unhappy about things." She picked up a small pebble and tossed it into the water. "I guess everybody gets that way sometimes. Dad says it's part of life."

Kyle lay down on his back and gazed up at the branches above them as they swayed in the wind. "He's right," he said. "I learned a long time ago that things don't always go the way you want them to. But if you can't do anything about it, you just have to accept it."

"Like not being a competitive skater any-more?" Holly blurted out, then slapped her hand over her mouth. "I'm sorry, Kyle—I shouldn't have said that. It just kind of slipped out."

Kyle sat up. "How did you know I used to compete?"

Holly avoided his eyes. "Well, for one thing, the way you skate. It takes time and good coaching to learn some of the things you can do, like—like a double axle, for in-stance. You couldn't have learned something like that if you just went to the skating rink on Saturday nights for fun."

"Maybe I'm just a fast learner," Kyle said.

Holly looked at him now. "No, Kyle. I know better."

"What do you mean?"

"Beth and I found your name in a national skating program. You don't go to Nationals unless you win at the regional level, and you don't win at Regionals unless you've got a coach and you're really good."

"So now you know," he said quietly.

"Why did you quit, Kyle?" Holly asked. "I know it's none of my business, but you're so good, and you seem to want to get even bet-ter or you wouldn't be asking me for help."

Kyle stared out over the lake. "It's very simple. Like you said, you have to have a coach, take lessons, pay dues, buy expensive skates. All that takes money, lots of money, and my folks just ran out of it."

All Holly could think of to say was, "I'm sorry."

"It's not your fault," Kyle said with a shrug. "It's nobody's fault really, but it's taken me forever to accept the way things are now. Sometimes it's hard to act as if everything's all right when it's really not."

Holly took Kyle's hand and looked into his eyes, filled with compassion and concern. "Want to talk about it?" she asked softly.

Kyle took a deep breath. "Yeah, why not? Got a couple of hours to kill?" he said with a faint smile.

"I've got all afternoon," Holly replied, letting go of his hand.

"A long time ago," Kyle began, "Dad was a competitive skater himself. He loved the sport and even after he and Mom were married and started raising a family, he continued to be active in it, teaching and helping out at one of the local rinks in his spare time."

A faraway look filled Kyle's eyes.

"He'd take me with him when I was a kid, and I learned to love skating, too. When I asked if I could give competitive skating a try, he agreed and became my coach."

"What a wonderful thing for your father to do!" Holly said. "From the way you skate, he must be a first-rate teacher as well as a great skater."

Kyle nodded. "He was. After I won my first meet, he gave me this."

Holly's eyes widened in awe as Kyle pulled a small medallion on a gold chain from under his shirt. She recognized it immediately. It was one of the medals given at the Pan-American Games, the highest award a roller skater could receive.

"How fantastic!" she murmured. "Did your father win this?"

"It's a replica," Kyle said. "The *real* medal Dad won is at home. It used to sit on the mantel in our living room, but now it's packed away." He glanced down at the medallion. "I'd always hoped one day to skate in the Pan-American Games like Dad, but that's out of the question now."

Holly put her hand on his arm. "Why? All you need is to start taking lessons again. . . ."

Kyle shook his head. "It's not that simple, Holly. You'll understand what I mean when I tell you the rest of the story." He took a deep breath. "We were living in Oklahoma when it happened. Dad worked in the oil fields for a small oil company, supervising the construction of oil rigs used at test sites.

100

One day he was working on a rig with a new design. He'd told his bosses he didn't think it would be stable, but they insisted the engineers knew what they were doing. So Dad's crew put it together.

"After they finished building it, Dad was still leery about the whole thing. Since he was responsible for any problems, he decided to check it out himself before giving the final go-ahead."

Holly could see Kyle's jaw tighten as he paused for a moment.

"He'd climbed about two thirds of the way up the frame when something snapped. He fell about forty feet to the ground. When it was all over, he had several broken ribs, a collapsed lung, and two crushed vertebrae."

Holly gasped. She'd heard about such tragic accidents, but she'd never personally known anyone involved in them. A broken finger was the worst catastrophe that had happened in her own family. "Oh, Kyle, that's awful," she whispered.

Kyle sat up. He picked up a small rock and threw it with all his strength far out into the lake. "There was an investigation by the company," he continued. "They said it was Dad's fault, that he hadn't followed the specifications outlined on the blueprints. At the time he was in no shape to argue with them, even though he knew he hadn't done anything wrong. He accepted what little money the company gave him and went on disability.

"After several months he was released from the hospital, but he's still confined to a wheelchair. A fellow worker told him about a doctor in this area who's had some success with patients suffering from severe back injuries like his. That's when my parents decided to move here."

He turned to Holly. "That's the whole story," he said. "With a younger sister and brother to feed and clothe, there isn't anything left over for luxuries like skating lessons—or much else, for that matter. So that's why I can't compete anymore."

"I—I don't know what to say," Holly mumbled.

"There's nothing to say." Kyle got up, pulling Holly along with him, and gave her a kiss on the cheek. "Let's go. I'm ready for some more of that lemonade your mom made."

That night, Holly tossed and turned as she lay in bed. She'd promised Kyle she wouldn't tell anyone, not even Beth, about his family's troubles. They didn't want people to pity them, or offer them charity.

Holly rolled over onto her stomach and punched the pillow with her fist, trying to find a comfortable position, but sleep wouldn't come. Finally, she got up and went over to her desk. She picked up the giraffe Kyle had won for her, holding it tightly as she sat down in the chair.

She sat there a long time staring at her trophy case and hugging the stuffed animal. *How would I feel if all my hopes and dreams were shattered in a split second?* she thought.

Chapter Eleven

The next afternoon at the rink, Holly skated around the floor, her mind light-years away.

"Hey, watch where you're going!" Beth said as she skated up beside her and grabbed her arm. "You almost ran into the wall. Are you okay? You've been out of it all day."

Holly blinked. "I'm fine. Just a little preoccupied, that's all."

"*I'll* say. How did everything go at the picnic? You and Kyle didn't have a fight or anything, did you?"

"Oh, no. We had a great time," Holly said.

"Did you ask him why he isn't competing anymore?"

Holly hesitated. "Sort of . . ."

"Well? What'd he say?" Beth asked.

"I can't tell you," Holly answered.

Beth came to a sudden stop in the middle of the floor and put her hands on her hips. "What do you mean you can't tell me? I'm your best friend, remember? If you can't tell your best friend, who *can* you tell?"

"Nobody," Holly mumbled. "Please, Beth. I promised Kyle I wouldn't talk about it to anyone."

"Boy, it must be something really awful if he doesn't want anyone to know," Beth said. "I can't imagine anything that could be that bad. Unless—"

Holly cut her off. "It's nothing really bad, honest. Let's just drop it, okay?"

"Okay—I guess. What choice do I have? But you *will* tell me as soon as you can, won't you?"

"As soon as I can," Holly promised.

For the rest of the week, Holly and Steve practiced every day after school, until their routine was nearly perfect. They were doing so well that Coach Gibson told them to take the day off on Friday, and Holly was glad for the break. She had seen Kyle only a few times since the picnic, and when they met, no more was said about his father's accident. Still, Holly couldn't forget about the problem.

She was sitting in class on Friday afternoon half listening to a lecture on the French and Indian War, wishing she could help Kyle realize his dream, when the door to the classroom opened. One of the secretaries from the office came in and handed a note to Mrs. Olson.

The teacher looked at the note, then glanced up at Holly, saying, "Holly, please stop by my desk after class. I have a message for you."

As Mrs. Olson proceeded with her lecture, Holly wondered what the message was. She figured it wasn't an emergency if it could wait until class was over.

As soon as the bell rang she jumped up from her chair and headed for Mrs. Olson's desk. Holly took the note from her teacher and hurried out the door. Opening the note, she quickly scanned the contents.

Coach Gibson called to say that your lesson with Steve tomorrow will be at 10:00 instead of 9:00.

I wonder why, Holly thought. *Oh well, I'll get to sleep in for a change.*

*   *   *

When Holly woke up and lazily rolled over on Saturday morning, she peered at the alarm clock on her night table. "Five minutes to nine!" she exclaimed. "Coach Gibson will kill me!" She started to leap out of bed, then remembered that her lesson was an hour later than usual. With a sigh of relief, she stretched her arms above her head. What a treat not to have to rush for once.

Holly was on her way to the bathroom when she heard the phone ring. A moment later her father shouted, "It's for you, Holly."

Probably Beth wanting a ride to the rink, Holly thought as she went back to her room and picked up the phone. "Hello?" she said, stifling a yawn.

A deep voice rumbled into her ear. "Holly, this is Coach Gibson. You had yesterday off, not today. You're late for your lesson with Steve. If you plan on skating in this meet, get down here pronto."

Before Holly could answer, he hung up. Dazed, Holly stared at the clock. It was only nine-fifteen. What was he talking about? She rummaged in her purse until she found the note she'd received the day before and carefully read it again. It still said ten o'clock. "What's going on, anyway?" she said aloud.

"Maybe the electricity went off for an hour during the night."

Holly ran to the head of the stairs and hollered, "Dad, what time is it?"

His reply confused her even more. "Nine-fifteen," he yelled back.

Holly hurried back to her room and quickly threw on a T-shirt and a pair of jeans. *No time for makeup today,* she thought, winding a rubber band around her ponytail. She grabbed her purse. Then remembering the note, she crammed it into her pants pocket and flew down the stairs.

"Where do you think you're going so fast?" her father said. "What about breakfast?"

"No time, Dad. I'm late for my skating lesson," she said as she hurried out the front door and jumped into her car. On the way to the rink, Holly's head was in a whirl. If Coach Gibson hadn't rescheduled her lesson, then who had sent her the message? Was this another prank someone was playing on her? She wondered if she should tell the coach about the strange things that had been happening lately. But what if he didn't believe her? What if he and Steve thought she'd just made it all up to excuse her being late again? Holly didn't want them to think she was unreliable or a liar!

Holly parked her car and hurried into the rink. Coach Gibson and Steve were waiting for her right inside the door, and neither of them looked happy.

Holly swallowed hard. "I'm really sorry," she said, looking from one stern face to the other. "But it wasn't my fault. You see, I got this message yesterday—"

Coach Gibson cut her off. "No excuses, Holly. Hurry up and change. Steve and I will be waiting for you on the floor—we've already been waiting for half an hour!"

Holly dashed down the aisle to Beth's locker, blinking back tears of anger and frustration. *It's not fair,* she said to herself as she dialed the combination. *He didn't even give me a chance to explain!* Grabbing her practice clothes and skates, she ran into the dressing room. Five minutes later, she was on the skating floor.

By some miracle, the lesson went extremely well, and by the end of it, both Coach Gibson and Steve were all smiles.

"Next Thursday night is the Skating Club meeting and dress rehearsal for the meet," Coach Gibson said. "Are your dresses about finished?"

"Almost," she replied.

"Good. How about your outfit, Steve?"

"All ready," he said.

"I want everyone here by six-thirty. *No later*," the coach said, eyeing Holly. "I'll post a note on the bulletin board. Make sure all the club members who are going to the meet know about it. Their parents are welcome to come also. If there are any problems, let me know."

"Right," Steve said, and Holly nodded.

As Coach Gibson headed for his office, Steve approached Holly. "Try to be a little more mature about your responsibilities, okay?" he said, then skated off toward his locker. Holly felt the frustration building inside her again.

As she stood gazing after Steve she felt a gentle tug on her ponytail. Whirling around, she saw Kyle grinning at her. "You almost got slapped," she said with a tight smile. "The way my morning's gone so far, you would have if you'd been anyone else!"

"What's the problem?" Kyle asked.

"Someone played another dirty trick on me this morning." She proceeded to tell Kyle what had happened.

"This has got to stop," he said, scowling. "If I ever find out who's doing it, they'll wish they hadn't."

Holly touched his arm. "I don't want you getting into any trouble on my account, Kyle. I know how much your job here at the rink means to you."

"I won't do anything dumb," he said. "But I *am* going to try to find out who's behind these so-called pranks."

Holly smiled at him. "Thanks. Well, guess I better practice my figures," she said. "I don't want the coach to think I'm slacking off."

"How about some lunch afterward?" Kyle asked.

"You're on! I didn't have time for breakfast."

"Meet you at your locker in an hour," Kyle said, then strode toward the back of the rink, whistling to himself.

The following week flew by for Holly. Her final rehearsal with Steve on Wednesday had been her best effort yet, and Coach Gibson hinted that a trophy was almost a sure thing.

When the bell rang on Thursday ending the school day, Holly and Beth hurried to the parking lot. Holly had a ton of things to do before dress rehearsal that night.

"I'm so *nervous*," Beth wailed. "What if I goof up, or fall, or forget the steps?"

Holly patted Beth on the back and laughed. "You say that about every meet, and it hasn't happened yet. Calm down!"

As they reached Holly's car, Beth walked

around to the driver's side. "Planning to drive today?" Holly asked, amused.

Beth groaned. "See?" she said. "If I can't even remember which side of the car I'm supposed to get in, how can I remember all those complicated routines?"

Beth's mother drove into the parking lot. "What's she doing here?" Beth cried.

Holly giggled. "You really are out of it! You've got a hair appointment this afternoon, remember?"

Beth gasped. "Oh, wow! I completely forgot! See you tonight!" She hurried over to where her mother was waiting for her.

Shaking her head, Holly started to open her car door.

"Hey, wait up," a voice shouted. It was Kyle. "I wanted to catch you before you left," he said, coming over to her. "I just wanted to wish you luck at the dress rehearsal tonight— not that you need it," he added with a grin.

"Thanks. But aren't you going to be there?" Holly asked.

"You bet," Kyle answered. "But I wanted to tell you now, in case I don't get a chance later. I know how confusing things can get. And I also know you're going to be terrific."

"I hope you won't be disappointed," she said.

"My only disappointment is that I won't be skating with you." Kyle reached for her hand and looked into her eyes for a long moment before saying, "Guess I'd better get going. Coach Gibson gave me a list a mile long of errands to run before tonight's rehearsal."

Holly smiled and watched him go over to his car and pull out of the parking lot before she got into her own car. As she started the motor, Holly saw the note she had taped to the dashboard earlier, reminding her to pick up her skates at the rink so she could polish them.

I'll do that right now, before I go home for my final costume fitting, she decided.

The rink was quiet and dim when Holly entered a few minutes after. As she started for Beth's locker, she noticed a shaft of light coming from the partially open door of the coach's office.

As Holly approached the office on sneakered feet, she heard someone talking. The male voice was vaguely familiar, but she couldn't identify it. Pausing just outside the door, Holly couldn't help listening.

"No. I won't do it. It's too dangerous—someone could get hurt," the person said. There was a pause, and Holly realized that whoever it was was talking on the phone. Then the voice said, "Holly never did any-

114

thing to you—it wasn't her fault that you broke your ankle." Another pause. "You can threaten me all you like, but I'm not going to play any more of your immature games. Good-bye, Valerie!" The speaker slammed down the receiver.

Holly gasped. *So Valerie was behind all those nasty tricks! But who's been doing her dirty work?*

Hearing footsteps inside the office, she silently flattened herself against the wall, blending in with the shadows as a tall figure stepped through the doorway. Just before he closed and locked the door behind him, Holly caught a glimpse of his face.

It was Craig Adams.

I should have guessed! Holly thought.

She stayed near the wall until Craig left the building. How she wished she could tell Kyle what she'd learned! But Holly didn't know where to find him. *I'll just have to wait until tonight,* she decided. But waiting was going to be very, very hard!

Chapter Twelve

When Holly, her parents, and Jeffrey entered the crowded rink that night, she immediately looked around for Kyle. She didn't see him, but she *did* see Valerie and Craig huddled in a corner. They seemed to be having a heated discussion. Holly was still angry at Valerie, but she also felt a little intimidated by the knowledge that Valerie would be watching her and Steve's routine.

Coach Gibson stepped up to a microphone at one end of the skating floor. "May I have your attention, please?" he said. Everyone stopped talking at the sound of his booming voice. "I'd like to welcome you all to the dress rehearsal for the Skating Club's upcoming meet," the coach went on. "After the rehearsal, you're all invited to stay for refreshments. And now, will the club members please change into their costumes?"

Holly and Beth hurried into the dressing room carrying their costumes and skates. "I'm so excited! Does my hair look okay? Drew hasn't seen it yet—I hope he likes it. Don't you just love our dresses? Aren't you excited, too?" Beth babbled.

Holly laughed. "Yes, I am. But I'm also a little nervous." For a moment she considered telling Beth about her discovery of that afternoon, but decided to wait until the rehearsal was over so she wouldn't ruin whatever was left of Beth's concentration on her routine. "By the way, have you seen Kyle anywhere?" she added. "I really have to talk to him."

"No, I haven't, but I'm sure he's around somewhere," Beth said, slipping into her dark green satin skating costume. "He wouldn't miss seeing you skate for anything. He's crazy about you, you know. Every time he looks at you, he gets puppy-dog eyes."

Holly blushed. "Oh, he does not!"

"Does, too." Beth zipped up the back of Holly's silver-trimmed turquoise dress. "And you look at him the very same way." Before Holly could protest, she said. "Come on—let's go warm up."

The girls joined the other brightly costumed skaters on the floor, and soon the dress rehearsal began. As Holly and Steve waited for their names to be called, Holly scanned the crowd for Kyle, feeling disappointed when she didn't see him. Then her eye fell on Valerie. She was sitting near the rail with her cast propped up in front of her, and there was a frown on her face. Holly thought Valerie's green eyes looked as cold as ice, and she shivered. *I have to show Valerie that her dirty tricks didn't have any effect on me at all,* she thought.

"Uh-oh—it's our turn," Beth whispered as Drew took her hand. "That means you and Steve are next!"

"Good luck!" Holly whispered back. "Knock 'em dead!"

The music Beth and Drew had chosen began to play, and Holly watched the couple glide onto the floor and breeze gracefully through their routine. When their performance ended, Holly clapped as hard as she could. Then she heard Coach Gibson announce her name and Steve's.

"This is it, partner," Steve said, smiling down at her. "Ready?"

"Ready as I'll ever be," Holly replied. She took his outstretched hand, and as they skated to the center of the floor, she finally saw the face she'd been looking for. Kyle was standing directly across from her by the rail, and when their eyes met, he grinned and gave her a thumbs-up.

Holly's heart leapt with joy. Swept away by the lilting rhythm of the dance music, she felt as if she were in a trance. The spins, jumps, and lifts she and Steve had struggled with for so long were second nature to her now. The two of them moved together in perfect harmony, their footwork strong and precise.

And then suddenly their routine was over, and she and Steve were bowing, hand in hand, while waves of applause washed over them. As they left the floor, Holly skated right into the open arms of her coach.

"You did it, Holly!" he said. "I knew you could." He grabbed Steve's hand and shook it vigorously. "Great work, both of you. If you guys skate like that at the meet, you'll have first place all sewed up!"

When the last skaters had finished their routines, Coach Gibson called them all into a circle. "I'm proud of every single one of you," he said. "And I'm confident that this meet is going to be our most successful one ever. Now go change clothes, and let's have a party!"

Holly was on her way to the dressing room when she saw Kyle waiting for her by the water fountain. To her amazement and delight, he strode over to her and put his arm around her.

"Congratulations on a great performance," he said huskily. "You were absolutely terrific."

"Thanks," Holly said, beaming. "But listen—I have something really important to tell you!"

"What is it?" Kyle asked.

Holly glanced around at the other skaters passing by. "Can't say right now. Can you meet me after I change?"

"Okay. I'll wait for you right here. Hurry back," he said, but since he was still holding her close, she couldn't move.

Holly giggled. "If you don't let me go, I *can't* hurry back," she pointed out.

"True," Kyle said with a grin, and reluctantly released her. "*Now* hurry back."

Holly made a dash for the dressing room. In less than five minutes, she had changed into her street clothes.

"What's the big rush?" Beth asked as she followed Holly out the door.

"Tell you later," Holly called over her shoulder.

True to his word, Kyle was waiting at the water fountain. "So what's the big secret?" he asked when she joined him.

Taking his arm, Holly led him farther down the hall. There were still a lot of kids and their families milling around, and she didn't want any members of the Skating Club to hear what she had to say. "Kyle, I know who's behind all those tricks on me."

He stared at her. "You're kidding! Who?"

"Valerie!" she announced.

"Valerie? But how? Until tonight, she hasn't been at the rink since she broke her ankle," Kyle said. "And even if she could have hobbled to your car on her crutches, I just can't see her messing up your engine."

"It was Craig who actually did all that stuff," Holly told him. "But Valerie put him up to it. When I came back to the rink this afternoon to get my skates, I heard him talking to her on the phone. I guess she'd asked him to do something else *really* mean, because he said he'd had it and hung up on her."

Kyle let out a long, low whistle. "You mean, Craig took your skate laces and changed your lock?"

Holly nodded.

"But how'd he get your lock combination? No one knew it but you and Beth."

"And Coach Gibson. Craig works here,

doesn't he? He probably slipped into the coach's office when nobody was paying any attention and looked in the files. And I'll bet he's the one who called school and told them my lesson was an hour later when it really wasn't," Holly said.

"I'll bet you're right," Kyle said. "He probably messed with the distributor cap on your car, too."

"But *why*?" Holly asked. "Why would Valerie have Craig do all those things to me?"

Kyle shrugged. "Maybe she was jealous."

"Jealous? Of me? She's a much better skater than I am—or she used to be before her accident."

"The question is, what are you going to do about it?" Kyle asked.

Holly frowned. "I don't know. I never thought about that."

"I think you should tell Coach Gibson," he said.

"No, I can't do that. If I do, I'm sure he'll kick her out of the club. And Craig will lose his job. I'd rather handle this myself."

Kyle put his hand on Holly's shoulder. "After all the things they did to you, she deserves it and so does he."

"There's got to be another way. . . . My dad always says the best way to solve a problem is to meet it head-on."

"Meaning?" Kyle asked.

"Why don't we confront them with what we know?"

"They'll just deny it."

"Maybe not. There's only one way to find out." She took Kyle's hand. "Let's go!"

When Holly and Kyle walked back into the rink, it was crowded with club members, their friends and parents, all enjoying the refreshments Coach Gibson had provided.

"I don't see them," Kyle said.

"There!" Holly pointed to the far corner of the rink. "See? Valerie's sitting by herself."

Kyle looked where she was pointing. "Oh, I see her. I wonder where Craig is?"

"I don't know, but let's start with her," Holly said, and they headed in Valerie's direction.

Holly marched up to Valerie and sat down in the empty chair next to her. "Hi. How's it going?" she asked brightly.

Valerie just shrugged.

"Where's Craig?" Kyle asked.

Valerie scowled at him. "Well, if it's any of your business, he went to get me something to drink. It's not easy moving around with *this* on your leg." She pointed to her cast. "But it'll be coming off before long, and then things will get back to the way they *should* be." She turned to Holly. "Coach Gibson sure gave you and Steve an easy routine for this meet. But that last spin could use some improvement," she said.

Holly saw a muscle tighten in Kyle's jaw. "Here comes Craig," he said.

"Yes, I can *see* even if I can't *walk*," Valerie snapped, taking one of the cups of soda Craig was carrying.

Craig took a swallow of his drink. "You did a real nice job tonight, Holly."

"Thank you," Holly replied, noticing the icy stare Valerie gave Craig.

There was a brief, uncomfortable silence. "We have something we'd like to discuss with you two," Kyle finally said.

"And what might that be?" Valerie said coolly.

Kyle looked straight at her. "We know all about those dirty tricks you both played on Holly."

"I have no idea what you're talking about," Valerie retorted. Craig didn't say anything at all.

"I think you do," Holly said.

Valerie turned to Craig. "Make these rude people stop their ridiculous accusations!"

Craig shook his head wearily. "Give it up, Valerie. I'm tired of you calling me your boyfriend just so I'd play your little games. I told you that earlier today, and I meant it." He looked over at Holly. "How'd you find out?"

"I heard you talking to Valerie on the phone this afternoon," she answered.

"So what if we played a few practical jokes? No harm was done," Valerie said.

"No harm?" Kyle echoed. "Maybe nobody was hurt, but Holly got in trouble with Steve and Coach Gibson several times. I think she should tell the coach everything."

Valerie looked at Holly. "Are you going to tell him?" she asked, her voice trembling slightly.

"I don't want to," Holly told her. "I know if I do, he'll kick you out of the club. But Valerie, *why*? *Why* did you do all those things?"

Valerie lowered her eyes. "I was—afraid."

"Afraid?" Holly repeated.

"Yes. Afraid you'd be so good that you'd take my dance partner away."

"Oh, Valerie, I'd never do that," Holly assured her. "Steve's *your* partner. You look so graceful when you're skating with him. You're the best team in the club—maybe in the whole state."

"You really mean that?" Valerie asked.

Holly smiled. "I sure do!"

A faint answering smile touched Valerie's lips. "Well, I must admit I was more than a little jealous tonight. You were really good, Holly."

"I appreciate the compliment," Holly said sincerely. "Someday I hope I'll be as good as you are."

"Maybe you will be," Valerie said with a touch of her old arrogance. Then she paused. "I'm really sorry about the things I made Craig do. I know it was stupid and mean. I wouldn't blame you for telling Coach Gibson."

Holly shook her head. "I'm not going to tell him, Valerie. As far as I'm concerned, it's over and done with. You're an important part of our club, and I don't want that to change."

Valerie's green eyes filled with tears. "Thanks, Holly," she whispered. Then she reached out and took Craig's hand. "I owe you an apology, too. Can you forgive me for being such a nasty witch?"

Craig looked down at her and smiled. "If Holly can, I guess I can, too," he said. He looked over at Holly. "But can you forgive *me*?"

"I already have," Holly said.

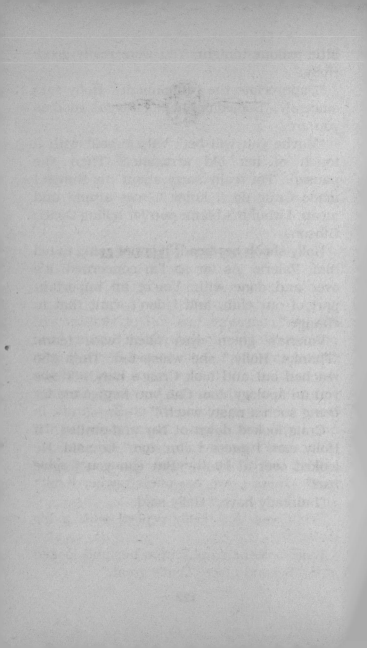

Chapter Thirteen

As the chartered bus full of skaters and parents returned to the rink on Sunday from the skating meet, Holly saw Kyle waiting in the parking lot. He blew her a kiss, and she returned it with one of her own. She ran down the steps holding the stuffed giraffe in one hand and a large silver trophy in the other, and raced over to where Kyle stood.

"You did it!" he shouted, giving her a big hug. "Guess I owe you one strawberry milk shake."

"That you do," Holly replied with a big smile.

Kyle took the trophy from her and looked at it. "Second place. That's great."

"The team that took first are going to be hard to beat," Holly said, "but I think Steve and Valerie will be able to do it."

Kyle wrapped his arm around Holly's waist while they waited for the luggage to be unloaded from the bus. "I've got some news for you, too," he said a little shyly.

"Oh? What is it?"

"Tell you later," he teased. "I need just the right setting. Like, maybe over a couple of milk shakes. How does seven o'clock tonight sound?"

Holly giggled. "Delicious!"

When Kyle and Holly entered the Burger Bar that night, the place was nearly deserted. Holly settled herself in a booth while Kyle ordered the shakes, her blue eyes glowing with anticipation. A few minutes later, Kyle returned. "One strawberry milk shake," he said as he placed it in front of Holly, then sat down next to her with his own drink.

"Well?" she asked eagerly. "Are you going to tell me your news now?"

Kyle grinned at her. "Dad's got a new job."

"That's wonderful!" Holly exclaimed. "But how—I mean, with his back injuries . . ."

"His spine will never be the same, but there's nothing wrong with his mind," Kyle told her. "The rehab program he's enrolled in helped him find the job. He'll be working as a consultant for a large architectural firm here in town. They're going to set him up with a computer and a modem so he can work right from our house."

"Oh, Kyle! Your family must be so thrilled."

"They sure are. It's been a long time since I heard my parents laugh—I'd almost forgotten what it sounds like. Dad's been wheeling around the house all weekend humming to himself." Kyle took Holly's hand and held it tightly. "Holly, you know what this means, don't you? I can start skating again."

Holly's eyes grew wide with excitement. "You can?"

"Yes. Dad and Mom gave their okay yesterday, and I had a long talk with Coach Gibson. He agreed to start my lessons this coming week." Kyle paused. "There's just one problem. . . ."

"What's that?" Holly asked anxiously.

He gave her a sly glance. "I need a partner for free dance. I thought maybe you could recommend someone."

"How about me?" Holly said, grinning from ear to ear.

Kyle's hazel eyes glowed. "I was hoping

that's what you'd say. Coach Gibson's already given his approval—he said it was up to you."

Holly threw her arms around his neck, her milk shake forgotten. "Oh, Kyle," she cried, "it's like a dream come true!"

Five weeks later, Holly and Kyle stood beside Coach Gibson, awaiting their turn to skate their free dance routine before the judges. Holly wore a dark blue skating costume studded with rhinestones, and Kyle's pants matched the color of Holly's dress. A white shirt and a dark blue bow tie completed his outfit.

"You look beautiful," Kyle said.

Holly smiled. "You look pretty handsome yourself."

"There's just one thing missing from your costume," he added.

Puzzled, Holly looked down at her dress. "What's that?"

Kyle reached into his pants pocket and took out the tiny gold medallion his father had given him long ago. He fastened the delicate chain around Holly's throat.

"Oh, Kyle!" she whispered. "I can't . . ."

He put his finger to her lips. "I want you to have it, Holly. It's very special to me, and now I want my special girl to wear it."

132

"Your—your special girl?" she repeated.

"Yes. I love you, Holly," he said, and then he kissed her tenderly on the lips.

"Oh, Kyle, I love you, too!" she murmured.

"Enough of that mushy stuff, kids," Coach Gibson interrupted with a grin. "You're on!"

The music began to play, and Holly looked into Kyle's eyes as he took her hand in his and led her onto the floor. She knew she was about to give the best performance of her life.

Sweet Dreams

SWEET DREAMS are fresh, fun and exciting —alive with the flavor of the contemporary teen scene—the joy and doubt of first love. If you've missed any SWEET DREAMS titles, then you're missing out on your kind of stories, written about people like you!